The Face of Trespass

by Ruth Rendell

THE FACE OF TRESPASS
SOME LIE AND SOME DIE
MURDER BEING ONCE DONE
A GUILTY THING SURPRISED
THE BEST MAN TO DIE
THE SECRET HOUSE OF DEATH
WOLF TO THE SLAUGHTER
A NEW LEASE OF DEATH
IN SICKNESS AND IN HEALTH
TO FEAR A PAINTED DEVIL
FROM DOON WITH DEATH

The Face of Trespass

RUTH RENDELL

PUBLISHED FOR THE CRIME CLUB BY
DOUBLEDAY & COMPANY, INC.
GARDEN CITY, NEW YORK
1974

R 292f

All of the characters in this book
are fictitious, and any resemblance
to actual persons, living or dead,
is purely coincidental.

ISBN: 0-385-01677-8
Library of Congress Catalog Card Number 73-10817
Copyright © 1974 by Ruth Rendell
All Rights Reserved
Printed in the United States of America
First Edition in the United States of America

I have peace to weigh your worth, now all is over,
    But if to praise or blame you, cannot say.
For, who decries the loved, decries the lover;
    Yet what man lauds the thing he's thrown away?

Be you, in truth, this dull, slight, cloudy naught,
    The more fool I, so great a fool to adore;
But if you're that high goddess once I thought,
    The more your godhead is, I lose the more.

Dear fool, pity the fool who thought you clever!
    Dear wisdom, do not mock the fool that missed you!
Most fair,—the blind has lost your face for ever!
    Most foul,—how could I see you while I kissed you?

So . . . the poor love of fools and blind I've proved you,
For, foul or lovely, 'twas a fool that loved you.

                                        Rupert Brooke

The Face of Trespass

BEFORE

The new Member of Parliament finished his after-dinner speech and sat down. He was not, of course, unaccustomed to public speaking but the applause of these men who had been his school fellows brought him a slightly emotional embarrassment. Accepting the cigar which the chairman of the Feversham Old Boys' Society was offering him covered for a moment this disturbance of his poise and by the time it was lit for him he was once more at ease.

"Did I do all right, Francis?" he said to the chairman.

"You were absolutely splendid. No platitudes, no dirty stories. Such a change to hear a crusader against social outrage! It almost seems a pity we don't have capital punishment any more so that you could abolish it."

"I hope I wasn't a prig," said the new Member quietly.

"My dear Andrew, you left-wingers always are, but don't let it worry you. Now do you want another brandy or would you like to —er, circulate?"

Andrew Laud refused the brandy and made his way to one of the tables where his former housemaster sat. But before he reached it someone tapped him on the shoulder and said, "Congratulations, Andy, on the speech and your success in the by-election."

"Jeff Denman," said the M.P. after a moment's thought. "Thank God for someone I know. I thought I was going to be stuck with old Scrimgeour there and that foul fellow, Francis Croy. How are you? What are you doing these days?"

Jeff grinned. "I'm fine. Now that I'm knocking thirty my family are getting over the disgrace of my driving a van for a living, so if you ever feel like moving house to live among your constituents I'll be happy to oblige."

"I might at that. Come and have a drink? You know, everyone here seems so *young.* I can't see a soul I know. I thought Malcolm Warriner might be here or that bloke David Something I used to have those fierce arguments with at the debating society."

"Mal's in Japan," said Jeff as they went up to the bar. "He'd be one of your constituents, as a matter of fact, if he were at home. Which brings me to one who isn't here but *is* a Waltham Forest constituent. Remember Gray Lanceton?"

The Member, to whose back this had been addressed, turned and emerged from the crush with two halves of lager in his hands. "He'd have been a year behind us. Tall dark bloke? Wasn't there a bit of a fuss when his mother remarried and he threatened suicide? I heard he'd written a novel."

"*The Wine of Astonishment*," said Jeff. "It was obviously auto-biographical, about a sort of hippie Oedipus. He shared my flat in Notting Hill with me and Sally for a bit but he didn't write anything more and when he started to feel the pinch he took Mal's place for somewhere to live rent-free. There was some sort of messy love affair too, I gather."

"He's living in my constituency?"

Jeff smiled. "You said 'my constituency' like a bridegroom saying 'my wife,' with shyness and great pride."

"I know. For weeks I've been thinking, suppose I lose the election and still have to come and talk to you a lot? What a fool I'd have felt. Does he like living there?"

"He says the Forest gets him down. I've been out there and I was surprised that there are such remote rural corners left only fifteen miles out of London. It's a weatherboard cottage he lives in at the bottom of a forest road called Pocket Lane."

"I think I know it," said the M.P., and reflectively, "I wonder if he voted for me?"

"I'd be very much surprised if Gray even knew there was a by-election, let alone voted. I don't know what's happened to him but he's turned into a sort of hermit and he doesn't write any more. In a way, he's one of those people you've committed your-self to help, the misfits, you know, the lost."

"I should have to wait till he asked for that help."

"No doubt you'll have enough on your plate without Gray Lanceton. I see Scrimgeour bearing down on us with the head-master in tow. Shall I melt away?"

"Oh, God, I suppose so. I'll give you a ring, Jeff, and maybe you'll come and have a meal with me at the House?"

The Member set down his glass and composed his features into that earnest and slightly fatuous expression which, generally reserved for babes in arms and the senile, seemed to do equally well for those pedagogues who had once awed him into terrified submission.

CHAPTER 1

It was sometime in early May, round about the fifth. Gray was never sure of the date. He had no calendar, he never bought a paper and he'd sold his radio. When he wanted to know the date he asked the milkman. The milkman always came on the dot of twelve, although he had no difficulty about knowing the time because he still had the watch she'd given him. He'd sold a lot of things but he wasn't going to sell that.

"What day is it?"

"Tuesday," said the milkman, handing over a pint of homogenised. "Tuesday, May the fourth, and a lovely day. Makes you feel glad to be alive." He aimed a kick at the young bracken shoots, hundreds of them all tightly curled like pale green question marks. "You want to get them ferns out of your garden, plant annuals. Nasturtiums'd do well there and they grow like weeds."

"Might as well keep the weeds."

"Them ferns'd get me down, but we can't all be the same, can we? Be a funny old world if we were."

"It's a funny old world now."

The milkman, who was easily amused, roared with laughter. "I don't know, you are a scream, Mr. L. Well, I must be off down the long long road that has no turning. See you."

"See you," said Gray.

The forest trees, which came very close up to the garden, weren't yet in full leaf but a green sheen hung over them, and this bright veil made a dazzlement against the sky. It was prematurely, freakishly hot. Gleaming in the sunshine, the beech trunks were the colour of sealskin. A good metaphor that, he thought, and thought too how once when he was a writer he would have noted it down for future use. Maybe some day, when he'd got himself

together and got some money and rid himself finally of her and
. . . Better not think of it now.

He'd only just got up. Leaving the front door open to let some
warmth and fresh air into the dank interior, he carried the milk
into the kitchen and put the kettle on. The kitchen was small and
very dirty with a slightly sunken floor of stone flags covered with
a piece of linoleum curling at its edges like a slice of stale bread.
All around him, as he waited for the kettle to boil, were those
kitchen appointments which had been the latest mod cons in
1890 or thereabouts, an earthenware sink, a disused range, an
enamel bathtub with a wooden cover on it. The kettle took a long
time to boil because it was coated with burnt-on grime and the
gas burner wasn't very clean either. Inside the oven it was even
worse. When he opened the oven door a black cavern yawned at
him. A good many times last winter, sitting in front of the
lighted oven in the Windsor chair, sitting in front of the black
cave with the gold-tipped blue flames quivering in its heart, he'd
been tempted to put out the flames, lay his head within that open
door and wait. Just wait for death—"Do something foolish," as
Isabel would put it.

He wouldn't do it now. The time for that was past. He would
no more kill himself over her than he would over his mother and
Honoré, and the time would come when he'd think of her as
he did of them—with irritable indifference. Not yet, though.
Memories of her were still in the forefront of his mind, lying down
with him at night, meeting him when he first woke, clinging to
him through the long empty days. He drugged them down with
cups of tea and library books but they were a long way from being
exorcised.

The kettle boiled and he made the tea, poured milk over a
couple of Weetabix and sat down to eat his breakfast on the bath
counter. The sun was high, the kitchen stuffy because the window
hadn't been opened for about a hundred years. Motes of dust
dancing in it turned the beam of sunshine into a solid shaft that
burned his neck and shoulders. He ate his breakfast in the des-
truction that wasteth at noonday.

This was her most usual time for phoning—this and, of course,
Thursday evenings. While he'd adjusted more or less to not seeing her, he still couldn't manage the problem of the phone. He

was neurotic about the phone, *more* neurotic, that is, than he was about other things. He didn't want to talk to her at all but at the same time he passionately wanted to talk to her. He was afraid she'd phone but he knew she wouldn't. When the tension of wanting and not wanting got too bad he took the receiver off. The phone lived in the horrible little parlour Isabel referred to as the "lounge." He thought of it as "living" there rather than standing or just being because, although for days on end it never rang, it seemed alive to him when he looked at it, vibrant, almost trembling with life. And when he took the receiver off on Thursday evenings, it seemed baulked, frustrated, peevish at being immobilised, its mouth and ears hanging useless from the dangling lead. He only went into the "lounge" to answer the phone—he couldn't afford actually to make calls—and sometimes he left the receiver off for days.

Finishing his breakfast and pouring himself a second cup of tea, he wondered if it was still off. He opened the "lounge" door to check. It was on. Saturday or Sunday he must have replaced it, turning the phone to stare at him like a squat, smug little Buddha. His memory had got very bad since the winter. Like an old man, he could remember the past but not the immediately recent past; like an old man, he forgot the date and the things he had to do. Not that there were many of those. He did almost nothing.

He opened the window on to the greening sunlit forest and drank his tea, sitting in an armchair covered with some early, perhaps the very earliest, prototype of plastic, a brown shiny fabric worn down to its cloth base at the arms and on the seat. There was only one other armchair. Between the two chairs was a low table, its legs made of moulded iron, its top burned by cigarettes from the days when he'd been able to afford cigarettes and marked with white rings from the base of the hot teapot. A stained Turkey rug, so thin that it wrinkled and rucked when he walked on it, lay in the middle of the floor. Apart from these, the only furnishings were Mal's golf clubs resting against the wall under the phone shelf and the paraffin heater on which she'd broken the perfume bottle and which, throughout the winter, had mingled her scent, evocative and agonising, with the reek of its oil each time it was lighted.

He pushed away the thought. He finished his tea, wishing he

had a cigarette or, preferably, a whole packet of twenty king-size. Almost hidden by the golf bag under which he'd concealed it, he could see the grey cover of his typewriter. It wouldn't be true to say he hadn't used it since he came to this cottage Mal called the hovel. He'd used it for a purpose he liked thinking about even less than he liked thinking about her, although the two were one and inextricably linked. To think of one was to think of the other. Better dwell instead on Francis's party, on getting away from this hole to London if only for a weekend, to meeting there some girl who would replace her—"with eyes as wise but kindlier and lips as soft but true, and I daresay she will do." To getting money together too, and finding a room, to sloughing off this dragging depression, this nothingness, even to writing again . . .

The phone gave the nasty little prefatory click it always made some ten seconds before it actually rang. Ten seconds were quite long enough for him to think in, to hope it was going to ring and at the same time to hope the click wasn't from the phone at all but from the worm-eaten floorboards or something outside the window. He still jumped when it rang. He hadn't learned how to control that, although he had managed to regard his reaction very much as a convalescent regards the headaches and tremors he still has. They will pass. His reason and his doctor have told him so, and meanwhile they must be borne as the inevitable aftermath of a long illness.

Of course it wasn't she. The voice wasn't husky and slow but squeaky. Isabel.

"You do sound tired, dear. I hope you're eating properly. I just rang to find out how things are."

"Just the same," he said.

"Working hard?"

He didn't answer that one. She knew he hadn't done a day's work, an hour's, for three years, they all knew it. He was a bad liar. But even if he lied and said he was working, that didn't help. They only asked brightly when "it" was coming out and what was it about and said how marvellous. If he told the truth and said he wasn't, they told him never to say die and would he like them to try and help get him a job. So he said nothing.

"Are you still there, dear?" said Isabel. "Oh, good. I thought they'd cut us off. I had a lovely letter from Honoré this morning.

He's really wonderful with your mother, isn't he? It always seems so much worse somehow, a man having to care for an invalid."

"Don't see why."

"You would if you had to do it, Gray. It's been a great blessing for you your mother having got married again and to such a wonderful man. Imagine if you had the looking after of her."

That was almost funny. He could scarcely look after himself. "Isn't that a bit hypothetical, Isabel? She married Honoré when I was fifteen. You might as well say, imagine if my father had lived or I hadn't been born or mother'd never had thrombosis."

As always when the conversation became what Isabel called "deep," she switched the subject. "What d'you think? I'm going to Australia."

"That's nice. What for?"

"My friend Molly that I used to have my typing bureau with, she lives in Melbourne now and she wrote and asked me. I thought I might as well go before I get past it. I've fixed on the beginning of the first week in June."

"I don't suppose I'll see you before you go," Gray said hopefully.

"Well, dear, I might drop in if I have a spare moment. It's so lovely and peaceful where you are. You don't know how I envy you." Gray gritted his teeth. Isabel lived in a flat over shops in a busy Kensington street. Maybe . . . "I always enjoy a quiet afternoon in your garden. Or wilderness," she added cheerfully, "as I should call it."

"Your flat will be empty, then?"

"Not a bit of it! The decorators are moving in to do a mammoth conversion job."

He wished he hadn't asked, for Isabel now began to describe, with a plethora of adjectives, precisely what alterations, electrifications, and plumbing work were to be undertaken in her absence. At least, he thought, laying the receiver down carefully on the shelf, it kept her off nagging him or harking back to the days when his life had looked promising. She hadn't questioned him about his finances or asked him if he'd had his hair cut. Making sure that the blether issuing distantly from the phone was still happily going on, he eyed himself in the Victorian mirror, a square of glass that looked as if it had just been breathed on or, possibly, spat on. The young Rasputin, he thought. Between shoulder-length hair and uneven beard—he'd stopped shaving at Christmas —his eyes looked melancholy, his skin marked with spots, the result presumably of a diet that would have reduced anyone less healthy to scurvy.

The mirrored face bore little resemblance to the photograph on the back jacket of *The Wine of Astonishment*. That had looked rather like a latter-day Rupert Brooke. From Brooke to Rasputin in five months, he thought, and then he picked up the phone again to catch the breathless tail end of Isabel's sentence.

" . . . and double glazing in every single one of my rooms, Gray dear."

"I can't wait to see it. D'you mind if I say goodbye now, Isabel? I have to go out."

She never liked being cut short, would have gone on for hours. "Oh, all right, but I was just going to tell you . . ."

Hollowly through the phone he heard her dog barking. That would fetch her. "Goodbye, Isabel," he said firmly. With a sigh of relief when she had finally rung off, he put his library books into a carrier bag and set off for Waltham Abbey.

Drawing a cheque to cash was the traumatic highspot of his week. For half a year he'd been living on the royalties he'd received the previous November, a miserable two hundred and fifty, drawing at the rate of four pounds a week. But that didn't take into account the gas and electricity bills he'd paid and Christmas expenses at Francis's. There couldn't be much left. Probably he was overdrawn already and that was why he waited, tense and uncomfortable by the bank counter, for the cashier to get up and, having flashed him a look of contempt, depart into some nether regions to consult with higher authority.

This had never happened and it didn't happen now. The cheque was stamped and four pound notes handed over. Gray spent one of them at the supermarket on bread and margarine and cans of glutinous meat and pasta mixtures. Then he went into the library.

On first coming to the hovel, he'd determined, as people do when retiring temporarily from the world, to read all those books he'd never had time for: Gibbon and Carlyle, Mommsen's

History of Rome and Motley's *Rise of the Dutch Republic*. But at first there had been no time, for she had occupied all his thoughts, and then when she'd gone, when he'd driven her away, he'd fallen back on the anaesthesia of old and well-loved favourites. *Gone With the Wind* would just about be readable again after four months' abstinence, he thought, so he got that out along with Dr. James's ghost stories. Next week it would probably be *Jane Eyre*, Sherlock Holmes, and Dr. Thorndyke.

The librarian girl was new. She gave him the sort of look that indicated she liked unwashed bearded men who had nothing better to do than loaf around libraries. Gray hazarded a return of the look but failed in mid-glance. It was no use. It never was. Her hands were stubby, the nails bitten. She had a ridge of fat round her waist and, while he was among the shelves, he had heard her strident laugh. Her lips were soft but she wouldn't do.

The books and the cans were heavy to carry and he had a long way to go back. Pocket Lane was a deep hole through the forest, a long tunnel to nowhere. The signpost at this end said LONDON 15, a fact which still amazed him. He was in the depths of the country but the heart of London was only fifteen miles distant. And it was quieter than the country proper, for here no men worked in the fields, no tractors passed and no sheep were pastured. A bright still silence, broken only by the twitter of birds, surrounded him. He wondered that people actually lived here from choice, voluntarily bought houses here, paid rates, *liked* it. Swinging his carrier bag, he passed the first of these houses, the Willises' farm—so-called, although they farmed nothing—with its exquisite lawns and florist's shop borders, tulips in red and gold uniforms standing in precise rows as if on parade. Next came Miss Platt's cottage, smart brother of the hovel, showing what fresh paint and care could do for weatherboard; lastly, before the rutted clay began and the forest closed in, the shuttered with-drawn abode of Mr. Tringham. No one came out to talk to him, no curtain moved. They might all have died. Who would know? Sometimes he wondered how long it would be before they found him if he were to die. Well, there was always the milkman . . .

The hawthorn hedges, fresh green and pearled with buds, ended at the end of the metalled road, and tall trees crowded in upon Pocket Lane. Nothing but bracken and brambles was strong enough to grow under the shade of those trees, in the leaf-mould crusted clay their roots had deprived of nourishment. Just at this point she had always parked her car, sliding it under the overhanging branches away from the eyes of those most incurious neighbours. How frightened she had always been of spies, of watchers existing only in her imagination yet waiting, she was sure, to relay her movements back to Tiny. No one had ever known. For all the evidence there was of their meetings, their love, none of it might ever have happened. The lush grass of spring had grown over the impress of her car tyres, and the fragile branches which had been broken by that car's passage were healed now and in leaf.

He had only to lift the phone and ask her and she'd come back to him. He wouldn't think of that. He'd think of *Gone With the Wind* and making a cup of tea and what to have for supper. It would be better to think about phoning her after six o'clock when, on account of Tiny, it would be impossible to do so, not now when it was practicable.

They said bracken made a comfortable bed and they were right. He lay on the springy green shoots reading, occasionally going into the hovel for fresh tea, until the sun had gone and the sky behind those interlaced branches was a tender melted gold. The birds and their whispered song disappeared before the sun and the silence grew profound. A squirrel slid down a branch onto the verge where it began to chew through the stem of a small doomed sapling. Gray had long ago got over thinking he was mad because he talked to squirrels and birds and sometimes even to trees. He didn't care whether he was mad or not. It hardly seemed important.

"I bet," he said to the squirrel, "you wouldn't mess about drinking tea or, in your case, eating plants, if you knew there was a beautiful lady squirrel panting for you not four miles away. You'd go right off and pick up the phone. You're not messed in your mind like humans and you wouldn't let a lot of half-baked principles get between you and the best lay in Metropolitan Essex. Especially if the lady squirrel had a whole treeful of luscious nuts stored away, now would you?"

The squirrel froze, its jaws clamped round the stem. Then it leapt up the trunk of an enormous beech. Gray didn't go near the phone. He immersed himself in the Old South until it grew too dark to read and too cold to lie any longer on the ground. The sky above him was indigo now but in the southwest over London a glowing plum-red. He stood by the gate as he always did at this hour on fine evenings, looking at the muted blaze of London.

Presently he went into the house and opened a can of spaghetti. At night the sleeping wood seemed to stir in its slumber and embrace the hovel entirely in great leafy arms. Gray sat in the Windsor chair in the kitchen under the naked light bulb, dozing, thinking, in spite of himself, of her, finally reading almost a third of *Gone With the Wind* until he fell asleep. A mouse running over his foot awakened him and he went upstairs to bed in the silent close blackness.

It had been a typical day, varying only in that it had been warm and sunny from the hundred and fifty or so that had preceded it.

CHAPTER 2

The post office, Gray thought, ought really to pay him a fee for causing them so little trouble. It couldn't be above once a week that the postman had to make the long trek down Pocket Lane to the hovel and then he brought only bills and Honoré's weekly letter. That had come on the previous Thursday in company with the gas bill, a demand for nine pounds which Gray didn't want to pay until he was more certain of his financial position. He'd be a whole lot more certain when he received from his publishers his royalty statement, currently due. It must be, he reflected, somewhere about May the twelfth or thirteenth now and surely that statement would arrive any day.

Meanwhile, he ought to write to Honoré before he did his shopping. *M. Honoré Duval, Petit Trianon*—God, he could never write that without squirming—*Bajon*, followed by the number that signified the department, *France*. He did the envelope first while he thought of what to say, always a difficult task. Two cups of tea had been drunk before he started. *Cher Honoré, Je suis très content de recevoir votre lettre de jeudi dernier, y inclus les nouvelles de maman* . . . His French was bad but no worse than Honoré's English. If his stepfather insisted on writing in a language of whose grammar and syntax he was abysmally ignorant—just, Gray was sure, to annoy—he would get as good, or as bad, as he gave. A few remarks on the weather followed. What else was there to say? Ah, yes, Isabel. *Imaginez-vous, Isabel va visiter Australie pour un mois de vacances* . . . *Donnez mes bons voeux à maman, votre* Gray.

That would shut him up for a bit. Gray took *Gone With the Wind* and the ghost stories and set off for the town where he posted his letter, bought half a pound of tea, a giant packet of Weetabix (this week's cheap offer) and two cans of Swedish meatballs. *Jane Eyre* was out and they'd only got one copy. He glowered at the fat girl, feeling ridiculously disappointed, almost paranoid. Didn't they realise he was one of their best customers? If Charlotte Brontë were still alive she'd be short of income through their incompetence. He took out *The Man in the Iron Mask* and the first of the Herries Chronicles, cast a glance of dislike at the grey pile of the Abbey, and walked gloomily back along Pocket Lane. A cigarette would have done a lot to mitigate the misery of these walks. Perhaps he could give up milk, cut down his tea, and use the resulting savings to buy forty cigarettes a week. Of course it was all absurd, this life. He could easily do something about it. Well, not *easily* but he could do something. Get a labouring job, for instance, or train as a G.P.O. telephonist. Half the telephonists in London were failed authors, broken lovers, unappreciated poets, intellectuals *manqué*. Only a little energy was needed, a scrap of drive . . .

The sun was unseasonably hot and, because of the humidity in this wooded place, unpleasant. In the shadowy gaps between the bushes gnats buzzed in clouds. Sparrows chattered, bathing in dust pockets in the dry clay of the path, and occasionally a jay screamed. The lane was sylvan, unspoilt countryside really, but it had something about it of a dusty room. And no matter what time of the year it was, the dead leaves lay everywhere, brown on the surface, falling to dust and decomposition below.

It was Friday, pay day, so the milkman was late, trundling back along the ruts, his work done.

"Lovely day, Mr. L. Makes you feel glad to be alive. May I trouble you for forty-two pee?"

Gray paid him, leaving himself with one, eighty, to last till he went to the bank next week.

"That's a couple of great books you've got there," said the milkman. "Studying, are you? Doing one of them external degrees?"

"The University of Waltham Holy Cross," said Gray.

"University of Waltham Holy Cross! You are a scream. I must tell the wife that one. Don't you want to know what day it is?"

"Sure. You're my calendar."

"Well, it's Friday, May the fourteenth, and I reckon you need reminding you've got a date. There's a car parked outside your place, one of them Mini's, red one. You expecting some beautiful bird?"

Isabel. "My fairy godmother," said Gray glumly.

"Best of luck, Cinderella. See you."

"See you—and thanks."

Bloody Isabel. What did she want? Now he'd have to find something to give her for her tea. You couldn't give a sixty-two-year-old Kensington lady ravioli or Weetabix at three in the afternoon. It was some months since he'd possessed a bit of cake. And she was bound to have brought that dog of hers, that Dido. Gray didn't at all dislike Isabel's Labrador bitch—in fact, he preferred her to her owner—but his godmother had a nasty way of forgetting to bring anything for the dog's evening meal and of raiding his meagre store of corned beef.

He found her sitting in the Mini's passenger seat, the door open. The Labrador was digging a hole among the bracken, snapping sometimes at the flies. Isabel was smoking a king-size cigarette.

"There you are at last, dear. I poked around the back a bit but you hadn't left a window open so I couldn't get in."

"Hallo, Isabel. Hallo, Dido. When you've dug that lot up you can get planting nasturtiums like the milkman said."

Isabel gave him rather a funny look. "Sometimes I think you're alone too much, dear."

"Could be," said Gray. Dido came up to him, got up on her hind legs and licked his face, putting her large, clay-filled paws around his neck. He thought she had a beautiful face, much nicer than most human faces—except one, always except one. Her nose was shrimp-pink and ice-cold. She had deep brown eyes—kind eyes, Gray thought, which was a funny thing to think about a dog. "I'll go and make us some tea." Dido, who was intelligent in matters of food, wagged her long frondy tail.

Isabel followed him. She pretended not to see the dirty plates or the flies and fixed her eyes on Gray instead.

"I won't ask you why you don't have your hair cut," she said, laughing merrily and sitting on the back step which she first dusted with her handkerchief.

"Good." Gray put the kettle on.

"No, but really, dear, you're not a teenager any more. Your hair's down on your shoulders."

"Since you're not going to ask me why I don't have it cut," said

Gray, "we may as well talk about something else. I'm afraid I don't have any cake. There's bread." He considered. "And Stork."

"Oh, but I brought a cake." Isabel creaked to her feet and loped off towards the car. A small fat woman, she wore turquoise trousers and a red sweater. Gray thought she looked like one of Honoré's garden gnomes. When she came back she was smoking a fresh cigarette. "I won't offer you one. I remember you said you'd given it up."

Experience should have taught him the cake wouldn't be the large homemade Dundee, marzipanned and iced, which he had been hungrily envisaging. He took the bakewell tart out of its packet. It was already in a foil case so he didn't bother with a plate. The dog walked in and shoved her nose between his hand and the bath cover.

"Now, darling, don't be tiresome." Isabel always called her dogs darling, reserving this endearment for canines exclusively. "Perhaps we could go into your lounge. I do like to sit down properly to my tea."

The phone was still off the hook from the night before. Tiny went to his masonic thing on Thursday nights and if she was going to phone, Thursday evening was the most likely time. Maybe she'd tried. Maybe she often tried on Thursday nights. He put the receiver back on the Buddha's knees, wondering what he'd say or do if she phoned now while Isabel was there. He fancied that today he could smell a faint breath of *Amorce dangereuse*, brought out perhaps by the warmth. Isabel watched him dealing with the phone. She preserved a tactful, heavily curious silence that was scarcely more endurable than her questions. She had armed herself, he noticed, with a box of tissues as might someone suffering from a heavy cold. Isabel didn't have a cold. She dusted the seat of her armchair with one tissue, spread another on her lap and asked him finally how he was getting on.

Gray had given up placating the old. It necessitated too many lies, too much elaborate subterfuge. Life might have been easier if he had deceived Isabel and Honoré into believing he was actually writing another novel, that the place was filthy because he couldn't get a cleaning woman, that he lived in Pocket Lane because he liked it. But he told himself that the approval of people he didn't himself approve of wasn't worth having so, accordingly, he replied that he wasn't, in the accepted meaning of the phrase, getting on at all.

"What a pity that is, dear. You were such a lovely little boy and you used to have such marvellous school reports. And when you got your degree your mother and I had such high hopes of you. I don't want to say anything to hurt you, but if anyone had asked me to predict your future in those days, I'd have said you'd be at the top of the tree by now."

"You won't hurt me," said Gray truthfully.

"And then you wrote that book. Not that I liked it myself. I don't care for books without a proper story. But all the people who know about these things forecast a wonderful career for you. And, oh, Gray dear, what has it come to?"

"Pocket Lane and Swedish meatballs," said Gray, blessing Dido for causing a diversion by sweeping her tongue across his plate.

"Take your face off the table, darling. Cake isn't good for doggies." Isabel lit a fresh cigarette and inhaled dizzily. "What you need," she said, "is some outside interest, something to take you out of yourself."

"Like what?"

"Well, that's really why I've come. No, I must be honest. I've come to ask you a favour but it would be very good for you as well. You'd admit you need something to do?"

"I'm not taking a job, Isabel. Not your sort of job, anyway. I can't be a clerk or a salesman or a market researcher, so can we get that clear from the start?"

"My dear, it's nothing like that. This isn't *paid*. It isn't a job in that sense. I only want you to do something for *me*. I may as well come straight to the point. What I want you to do is look after Dido for me while I'm in Australia."

Gray said nothing. He was watching a fly which was either eating, or laying eggs on, a lump of icing that had fallen onto the rug. Dido was looking at it too, her eyes going round in wild circles when the fly rose sluggishly from the crumb and drifted about in front of her nose.

"You see, dear, I've never left her since she was a puppy and she's five now. I couldn't put her in kennels. She'd fret and I shouldn't enjoy myself knowing she was fretting."

London, Kensington, just to get away, and so easily. "You mean, look after her in your flat?"

"No, dear. I told you I was having builders in. Look after her here, of course. She loves it here and your not having a job means she wouldn't be left alone. You could take her out for lovely walks."

It wouldn't be too bad, he supposed. He liked Dido better than he liked most people. And Isabel would provide her food with possibly a little extra in the shape of actual money.

"How long for?"

"Just four weeks. I go on Monday, June the seventh. My aircraft leaves Heathrow at three-thirty. What I thought was I could bring Dido to you on the Sunday evening."

"Sunday, the sixth?"

"That's right."

"Sorry, Isabel," said Gray firmly. "Not possible. You'll have to find someone else."

He wasn't going to give up Francis's party, especially for Isabel. Francis's party was the only thing he had to look forward to, the only thing that kept him going, he thought sometimes. He'd planned ahead for it, deciding to go up on the Sunday morning, wander round the Park, look at the street vendors in the Bayswater Road and arrive at Francis's by about four. That would mean helping to get food ready and hump crates of booze, but he didn't mind that, particularly as it would get him into Francis's good books and secure him the offer for a bed for the night. Well, not the night but the period of from five in the morning till he woke up somewhere around noon. He had had fantasies about this party, real people to talk to, unlimited drink and cigarettes, the new girls, one of whom might be the one to make him forget and with whom he might even share that bed or couch or carpet or patch of floor. The idea of sacrificing this for anything less than severe illness or his mother's dying or something equally seismic made him feel almost sick.

"Sorry, but I'm doing something that Sunday."

"Doing what? You never do anything."

Gray hesitated. It was one thing to resolve not to placate the old, quite another to stick this system out. He could tell Isabel he'd be dining with his publishers but that was improbable on a Sunday night and, knowing he hadn't published anything for three years, she was unlikely to believe it. Again he decided on the truth.

"I'm going to a party."

"On a *Sunday?* Oh, Gray dear, I do find that strange. Unless you're going to see someone there you might—well, who might give you a helping hand?"

"Very possibly," said Gray, thinking of the imaginary girl. Not wanting to be jesuitical, he added, "This party's just for pleasure, no strings. But I want to go. I'm sorry, Isabel, I see you think it's selfish and maybe immoral—yes, you do—but I can't help that. I'm not putting off this party for you or Dido or anyone."

"All right, dear, don't. I can manage to bring Dido the next morning. I can bring her at twelve and go on from here to the airport."

Christ, he thought, that was persistence for you. No wonder she'd made a fortune bludgeoning executives into employing her illiterate little typing pool rejects.

"Isabel," he said patiently, "this is not going to be a cocktail party where nice middle-aged fuddy-duddies eat twiglets and drink martinis from six till eight. This is going to be more in the nature of an all-night orgy. I shan't get to bed till five or six and, naturally, I shan't want to leap up again at nine to get back here and re-ceive you and your dog."

"You're very frank!" Isabel tossed her head and coughed in a futile effort to prevent his seeing how deeply she had blushed. "I should have thought a little natural shame about carryings-on of that kind wouldn't be out of place. You might have had the de-cency to think up some excuse."

They didn't even want you to be truthful. They knew you liked sex and liquor—in fact, they thought you liked them a hell of a lot more than you did—but you were supposed to put up some Vic-torian pretence that a simple Westbourne Grove rave-up was really a conference at the Hyde Park Hotel.

"Can I have one of your cigarettes?"

"Of course you can. I would have offered, only I thought you'd given it up. Now, dear, why shouldn't I bring Dido here at twelve and just put her in the house—shut her in the kitchen, say, till you get home?"

"O.K., you can do that." There was evidently no escape. "I'll be back around three. I suppose she'll be all right for three hours?"

"Of course she will. I'll leave her some water and I'll leave you enough tins and money for fresh meat to last you out." Isabel went off into a long string of instructions for Dido's proper care while the dog, unobserved by her owner, though not by Gray, removed the remains of the bakewell tart from the table. "Now what about a key?"

When he first came to the hovel there had been three keys. One he carried about with him, one hung on a nail above the kitchen sink, and the third—probably she had thrown it away by now, along with anything else she had to remember him by. Gray went out and fetched the spare key.

"I'll shut her in the kitchen because, though she's very clean *normally*, she might have a little accident if she's alone in a strange place."

Gray said that little accidents would make small difference to the general grot in the hovel, but he agreed to this, telling Isabel the kitchen window didn't open.

"That won't matter for three hours, as long as you make a fuss of her when you come in and take her for a nice walk. I'll put the key back on the hook, shall I?"

Gray nodded. While Isabel wiped her mouth and brushed her lap with fresh tissues, he put out his hand to the dog who gambolled over at once, licked his fingers and sat down beside him, leaning her soft golden weight against his knees. He let his arm fall over her as it might encircle a woman's shoulders. The warmth of flesh, of blood pulsing, was a strange sensation to him, new in a way. This wasn't human flesh and blood; there was no infinity of mind under that shapely skull. But the very touch of warmth and the pressure of what seemed like real affection, brought him a sudden sharp pain, brought home to him the agony of his loneliness. And at that moment he was terribly near to tears for loss, for unconquerable apathy, for waste, and for his own feeble self.

But it was in his normal voice that he said, "We'll be all right, won't we, Dido, my old love? We'll get on fine."

Dido lifted her head and licked his face.

CHAPTER 3

At some sleepy hour, about eight perhaps, he heard a letter flop on to the front door mat. It couldn't be another one from Honoré, not yet. The electricity bill—too small to distress his bank account —was paid; the final demand for the gas wasn't due yet surely. It must be that royalty statement at last. And about time too. Not that it would announce some huge windfall, but if it was only a hundred, only fifty . . . Just a tiny bit of capital like that would give him the incentive to get away from here, find a room in London, take a job working a bar or washing up till he got himself together to write again.

The bedroom was filled with pale light, moving as wind tossed the beech branches. He lay there, thinking about London, about Notting Hill, Ladbroke Grove switchbacking up to Kensal Green, people in the streets all night. No branches, no clay, no leaves crepitating and rustling wherever you walked, no more vast blank days. Although he didn't expect to sleep again, he dozed off into a dream—not of London, as might have been expected, but of her. In the weeks following their separation he had dreamed of her every night, had been afraid to sleep because of those dreams, and they still came often, once or twice a week. Now she was in the room with him, this very room, the wind blowing her hair that was neither red nor gold nor brown but a fox fur blend of all three. And her eyes, the colour of smoky crystal, were on him.

She said, holding out a little hand the rings shackled, "We'll talk about it. There's no harm in just talking."

"There's no point either."

She didn't listen to his reply. Perhaps he hadn't made it aloud. Who knows in dreams? "It's been done before," she said. "Lots of people in our sort of situation have done it. You'll say they got caught." He said nothing, only gazed into those eyes. "You'll say

that, but we don't know about all the ones who didn't get caught.
They're the kind we'll be."

"We?" he said. "The kind we'll be?"

"Yes, darling, yes, Gray . . ." Closer now, her hair blown against
his skin. He put out his arms to hold her, but her flesh was hot
and that flying hair flames. He shrank, pushing away the fire, crying out as he surfaced from the dream, "I couldn't do it, I couldn't
kill a fly . . . !"

There was no staying in bed after that. Shivering from the effect
of her presence—for is a dream woman less a presence than a real
one?—he got up and pulled on jeans and faded T-shirt. Gradually
his body stopped shaking. Reality splashed back in hard light and
loneliness and the dull hopeless safety of being without her. He
looked at his watch. Half-past eleven. He wondered what day it
was.

Almost the first thing he saw when he got downstairs was a
cow's face, white and gingery-brown, looking at him through the
kitchen window. He opened the back door and went out into the
patch of stinging nettles, birch saplings and hawthorn that was
supposed to be a garden. It was full of cows milling about under
the sagging greyish washing he'd left hanging on the line since
Sunday. The Forest wasn't fenced and farmers could let their cattle wander about as they pleased which was a cause of misery and
frustration to the garden-proud. Gray approached the cows, pat-
ting several of them on their noses which had much the same feel
as Dido's, and addressing them aloud on the virtues of anarchy
and contempt for property. Then he remembered the letter, the
royalty statement, and he went in to fetch it. But before he picked
it up, the stamp on the envelope—that bloody affected Marianne
strewing flowers or whatever—told him he'd been wrong.

"My dear son . . ." Gray was used to that by now but it still
made him wince. "My dear son, I try to telephone to you Thursday last evening but the line is occupied and again Friday and the
line still occupied. How gay the life you have with many friends!
You must not be unquiet but mummy is again not well and the
doctor Villon say she have an other attack of paralyse. There is
much work here for me who is habituate to be just a poor infirmier
and work all day and night making care of your mummy.

"Now it will be good if you come. Not today I mean but be

ready to come if mummy is not so well. For that when you must come I will talk to you with the telephone to tell you now is the time you must come my son. You will say you have no money to pay the train or the avion company but I will send you the money not in a letter as that is against law which I will not but to your bank that is Midland in Waltham Abbey as you have said where you can take it when you must come. Arrangements for this I make. Yes you say this is funny. Honoré pay money to me when he is caring so for his little saved money but old Honoré know the duty of a son for his mummy and for this he break the rule of sending no money to a son who work not at all and make arrangement for the bank to have thirty pounds of money.

"Do not be unquiet. Doctor Villon say the good God take mummy not yet and no need to send to Father Normand but tell you who is her one son and child. Be calm my boy. Your loving papa Honoré Duval. P.S. I have borrowed to the mayor the french traduction of your book you have gave me and he read when he has leisure. You will like to have the critique of a man of reason what the mayor is. H.D."

Gray knew that the Mayor of Bajon's sole claim to literary judgment was the fact of his great-aunt's having been maid to a cousin of Baudelaire. He screwed the letter up and threw it behind the bath. Honoré knew perfectly well he could read French without difficulty but he insisted on writing in the horrible dining-room English he had picked up while a waiter in Chaumont. Gray didn't suppose his mother's life was really in danger and he wasn't prepared to rely on the word of Dr. Villon, another one of Honoré's cronies along with the mayor at Bajon's local, the Écu d'Or.

He wouldn't go so far as to say he didn't care whether his mother lived or died, and he certainly intended to fly over to France if she were really on her deathbed, but he hadn't much feeling for her left. It would be false to say that he loved her. It had been a great shock to him when, touring through France with Isabel, his mother had fallen in with—Gray wasn't prepared to say fallen in love with—one of the waiters at the Chaumont Hotel. He had been fifteen, his mother forty-nine and Honoré probably about forty-two. Honoré even now never revealed his true age, making out he was a poor old man on whom the duties of nursing weighed heavily. They had got married very quickly after that, Honoré being well aware, Gray knew, that his betrothed owned the car she was travelling in as well as, far more important, a fairly large house on Wimbledon Common. Whatever its effects on the bride's relatives, the marriage had apparently worked out wisely and well. The Wimbledon house had been sold and Honoré had built a bungalow in his native village of Bajon-sur-Lone, where they had lived ever since. Mme. Duval had become a Catholic on her marriage, another departure which Gray found hard to forgive. He had no religion himself, largely due to his mother's having taught him agnosticism from his cradle. All that had gone when she remarried. Now she had the priest to tea and put ashes on her forehead on *mercredi des Cendres*, or had done when she had been well enough. The first stroke had hit her four years before. Gray had gone over then, paying his own fare out of money earned by selling short stories, and again when she had the next one, relying this time on part of the handsome advance on his novel. Sometimes he wondered how he was going to make it when the *attaque de paralyse* struck again, perhaps fatally. Now he knew. Honoré would stump up.

Honoré *had* stumped up. It was quite pleasant to think of the money being there, waiting for him, making his own waiting for that statement less fraught with worry. He mixed some packet curry with water, heated it in a saucepan and ate it on the front doorstep while watching the cows who had begun to wander off in search of richer pastures than Mal's nettle bed. At twelve sharp the milkman arrived.

"I've got my own dairy," said Gray, who sometimes felt obliged to live up to his reputation as an entertainer. "You'd better watch out or you'll find yourself redundant."

"Got your own dairy? You're a real comedian, you are. Them cows is all bullocks, or hadn't you noticed?"

"I'm just a simple Londoner and proud of it."

"Well, it takes all sorts to make a world. Wouldn't do if we was all the same. Just for the record, it's Thursday, May the twentieth."

"Thanks," said Gray. "See you."

"See you," said the milkman.

Gray did a mammoth wash-up, his first for four or five days, read the last chapter of *Rogue Herries* and set off down the lane. Rain had fallen at the beginning of the week and the clay was soggy, churned up by the hooves of the twenty or so bullocks who had left behind them steaming pats of dung from which rose a sour scent. He caught up with them outside the gate to the farm. He didn't know much about Willis except that he had a hatchet-faced wife and a red Jaguar. But cows live on farms; these cows evidently wanted to get into this farm; obviously it was the place for them. He opened the gate, a fancy affair of cartwheels stuck between bars, and watched the cows canter clumsily in the way cows have, up the gravel drive and across Mr. Willis's lawn. This was a sheet of glistening green velvet onto which a sprinkler scattered a fine cascade of water drops. He leant against the gatepost, interested by the cows and amused at their antics.

Three of them began immediately to devour tulips, stalks, and vermilion blooms sprouting from their jaws in a way that Gray thought rather delightful and reminiscent of some Disney cartoon. The others jostled each other about the lawn and one began to make its way round the back of the house. He was just moving off again, shifting his books to his other arm, when a bedroom window of the farmhouse was flung open and a voice screamed at him:

"Did you open that gate?"

The hatchet-faced Mrs. Willis.

"Yes. They wanted to come in. Aren't they yours?"

"*Ours?* When did we ever keep cattle? Can't you see what you've done, you stupid man? Look what you've done."

Gray looked. The exquisite moist turf was mashed by the indentations of some eighty cloven feet.

"I'm sorry, but it's only grass. It'll heal up or whatever the right term is."

"Heal up!" yelled Mrs. Willis, leaning out and shaking her arms at him. "Are you mad? D'you know what it's cost my husband to get his lawn like that? Years and years of labour and hundreds of pounds. You ought to be made to pay for what you've done, you—you long-haired layabout. I'll see to it my husband makes you pay if he has to take you to court."

"Oh, piss off," said Gray over his shoulder.

Screeches of reproach, threats of retribution and of shocked disgust at his language pursued him down the lane. He felt rather cross and shaken, a state of mind which wasn't improved by finding, when he got to the bank five minutes before they closed that he had just two pounds, forty-five pence in his account. This he drew out, remembering Honoré's thirty which should arrive any day. It wouldn't do, however, to splash out on any fancy tins. He returned *Rogue Herries* and *The Man in the Iron Mask* and took out *Anthony Absolute*, *The Prisoner of Zenda*, and *No Orchids for Miss Blandish*, all in paperback treated with the sort of fortifying process the library went in for. They were light to carry and on the one day he didn't need a lift he got one. He had just entered Pocket Lane when Miss Platt's car pulled up beside him.

"I'm so glad I saw you, Mr. Lanceton, because I want to ask you if you'll come to my little party on Tuesday fortnight."

Gray got into the car. "Your what?" he said. He hadn't meant to be rude, for he liked what he knew of Miss Platt, but the idea of anyone of seventy giving a party and out here was so novel as to be shocking.

"Just a few friends and neighbours in for drinks and a sandwich at about seven on June the eighth. I'm moving, you see. I've sold the house and I'm moving out on the ninth."

Gray muttered something about being sorry to hear that. They passed the farm which the cows had now left. Mrs. Willis was on the lawn, prodding at the broken turf with a rake.

"Yes, I sold it the same day I advertised it. Really, I thought the price the agent told me to ask was quite ridiculous—fifteen thousand pounds for a cottage! Can you imagine?—but the man who's bought it didn't turn a hair."

"It's a lot of money," Gray said. He could hardly believe it. Miss Platt's place was just like the hovel, only smartened up a bit. Fifteen thousand . . .

"House prices have trebled around here in the past few years. The Forest can't be built on, you see, and yet it's so near London. I've bought the flat above my sister's in West Hampstead because she's really getting past looking after herself. But it seems dreadful after this lovely spot, doesn't it?"

"I wouldn't say that," said Gray sincerely. "You'll have a great time."

"Let's hope so. But you will come?"

"I'd like to." A thought struck him. "Will the Willises be there?"

"I haven't asked them. Are they particular friends of yours?"

"I think Mrs. Willis is my particular enemy. I let the cows into her garden."

Miss Platt laughed. "Oh, dear, you must be unpopular. No, there'll just be me and my sister and Mr. Tringham and a few friends from Waltham Abbey. Do you often hear from Malcolm Warriner?"

Gray said he'd had a postcard with a picture of Fujiyama at Easter, thanked Miss Platt for the lift and got out. He made a pot of tea and sat in the kitchen reading *The Prisoner of Zenda* and eating slices of bread and Stork. The wind had risen, blowing the clouds and making the place quite dark, though it was still early. He lit the oven and opened it to give him some warmth.

It wasn't till the phone started ringing that he remembered the milkman had said it was Thursday, the night he always took the receiver off. His watch said ten past seven. Tiny would have been off to his masonic thing an hour ago. Every Thursday night she tried to get him, but she'd never been able to because the receiver was always off. It wasn't off tonight and she was succeeding. Of course it was she. She would speak to him, he would speak to her, and in half an hour she would be here. He moved towards the "lounge," the phone, not rushing but walking slowly and deliberately as a man may walk to an inevitable, hated, yet desired, fate. His heart was thudding, it actually hurt. She was in that phone like a genie in a lamp, waiting to be released by his touch, to flow into and fill the room, red-gold, crystal green, *Amorce dangereuse.*

He was so certain it was she that he didn't say hallo or give Mal's number but said what he'd always said when he knew it was she phoning, "Hi," miserably, resignedly, longingly, in a very low voice.

"Gray?" said Francis. "I want to speak to Graham Lanceton."

Relief? Despair? Gray hardly knew what he felt unless it were the beginning of a coronary. "This is me, you fool. Who did you think it was? D'you think I keep a staff?"

"It didn't sound like you."

"Well, it was. It is."

"Really, this is getting ridiculous. You sound as if you're messing your mind properly out in that dump. Look, I'm phoning about this party. Could you possibly come up on the Saturday?"

Ten minutes before he'd have been excited at the very idea. "Yes, if you like," he said.

"I've got to meet this aged relative at Victoria on the Saturday morning and I want someone to be here when the blokes come to fix up some rather fancy electric wiring I'm having done for the party. A sort of blink arrangement that has quite an alarming psychedelic effect."

"I'll be there. I can get to you by ten." His heart had stopped pounding. As he put the phone down, he felt limp, sick. He sat in the brown plastic armchair, in the dusk, and stared at the silent secretive phone, the detached self-confident phone that had snapped shut its organs like a sea anemone, and squatted on its seat, not returning his gaze but withdrawn now as if it were asleep.

Christ, but he mustn't start investing the thing with a personality. That was real neurosis. That could lead to only one end, to a ward in a mental hospital and E.C.T. or something. Better anything than that. Better dial her number now, talk to her, establish once and for all that there was never again to be any contact between them.

But they'd established that at Christmas, hadn't they?

"If you phone me, I'll put the receiver down."

"We'll see about that," she'd said. "You wouldn't have the will power."

"Don't try me then. I've told you till I'm sick of it, if you can't leave off getting at me about that obsession of yours, it's no use any more. And you can't obviously."

"I do what I want. I always do what I want."

"All right, but I don't have to do what you want. Goodbye. Go away now, please. We shan't see each other again."

"You're bloody right there," she'd said.

So it had been a pact, hadn't it? I've loved you faithfully and well two years or a bit less, it wasn't a success . . . If it had been a pact, why did he hope and fear? Why did he take the receiver off? Because she'd been right and if she phoned he wouldn't have the will power to resist. Because he knew confidently, proudly, that five months separation wouldn't be long enough to stop her loving him. But, as a woman, maybe she wouldn't risk the humiliation of phoning him and being repulsed. He could phone her . . .

Tiny wouldn't be home before eleven. She was alone there, he alone here. It was all ridiculous. He was making himself ill, ruining his life. He jerked out of the chair and stood over the phone.

Five-O-eight . . . He dialled that bit fast but paused before going on with the rest of the number, the four digit bit. Then he dialled it more slowly, dialled three of the numbers. He inserted his finger in the nine hole, let it linger there, trembling, pulled it out with a soft "Oh, Christ" and banged the side of his hand down on the receiver rest. The receiver dropped, swinging, knocking against the golf clubs.

It wasn't any good. For one evening, maybe for a whole week, he'd have her in peace, but it would start again, the nagging, the one topic of conversation that filled the spaces between lovemaking. And he couldn't keep on stalling the way he'd stalled last summer and last autumn because in the end he'd have to tell her he couldn't do it. He'd have to say, as he'd said at Christmas, that if it was doing that or not seeing her he'd choose not seeing her.

He went out of the front door and stood among the bracken the cows had flattened into a prickly mattress. Black branches whipped against a sky of rushing cloud. Over there, behind him, lay Loughton, Little Cornwall, Combe Park. It was ironic, he thought wearily, that he was longing for her and she for him, that only four miles separated them, that the phone would link them in a second; that neither had qualms about betraying Tiny or revulsion for adultery, but they could never meet again because she wouldn't stop demanding what he wouldn't do, and he couldn't, under any circumstances, agree to do it.

CHAPTER 4

He didn't sleep much that night. Probably this was due to his not following his usual sleep-inducing method, the writer's resource, of telling himself a story as soon as he laid his head on the pillow. Instead, he did what he'd done those sleepless nights of January, thought about her and their first meeting.

Yet he'd hardly intended to get on to it. He lay there, examining the curious results of haphazard chance, how some tiny alteration of purpose or a word spoken by a friend, a delay or a small change in the day's routine, may ineluctably dictate the course of a life. Such had happened when his mother and Isabel, awakened in the small hours by the phone ringing—a wrong number, of course—and unable to sleep again, had set off earlier than they'd intended and reached Dover in time to catch the first boat. Because of this they were down as far as Chaumont by the evening, although they shouldn't really have been there till the next night when Honoré would have been off duty. Who had made that phone call? What careless unthinking arbiter had misdialled at four in the morning and so made a marriage and changed a nationality?

In his own case, he knew his arbiter's identity. Jeff had helped himself to the last twenty sheets of typing paper—for what? To make out some removals bill? Some list of household goods?—and he'd had to go out to Ryman's and get a fresh ream. The branch in Notting Hill were out of stock. Why hadn't he walked across the Park to the branch in Kensington High Street? Because the 88 bus had stopped at the red light. At that moment the traffic lights had turned red, the bus had stopped and he had got on it. So was it the light that had made his fate, or the buyer who hadn't got the paper in, or Jeff, or the householder who had to have a list of tables and chairs made before he could move? Useless to go on.

You could get back to Adam that way, back and back, trying to learn who spun, who held the scissors and who cut the thread.

The 88 took him down Oxford Street and he'd gone to Ryman's in Bond Street. He'd always felt good with a fresh ream of paper under his arm. It wasn't daunting but a challenge, that virgin pack he would fill with richness. And because he'd been dwelling on this, looking down and not where he was going, he'd crashed into her before he even saw her face, cannoned right into the girl who was walking towards him, so that her parcels tumbled on to the pavement and her scent bottle broke against a shop window ledge.

He could smell it now, the same smell that had lingered so long in the hovel. It rose in a hot heady cloud, steaming on the crisp January air.

"Can't you look where you're going?"

"The same applies to you," he'd said, not very politely, and then, softening because she was beautiful, "I'm sorry about your perfume."

"So you bloody should be. The least you can do is buy me another bottle."

He shrugged. "O.K. Where do we get it?" He thought she'd refuse then, say it didn't matter. The impression he had of her as they stood close together, picking up parcels, was that she wasn't at all badly off. A red fox coat, the same colour as her hair, cream leather boots—at least thirty quids' worth—rings bulging through the fine leather gloves.

"In here," she'd said.

He didn't mind. At that time, though not rich, he was richer than he'd ever been before or since. He followed her into the hot crowded store, holding his small square packet of paper.

"What's it called, that stuff of yours?"

They were at a vast series of cosmetic counters.

"*Amorce dangereuse.*"

It cost him nearly six pounds. The price was so ridiculous, her childlike simple acceptance of it so straightforward—she smiled happily, dabbed some of it on his wrist as well as on her own—that he burst out laughing. But he stopped laughing abruptly when she brought her face close to his, laid a hand on his arm and said, whispering, "D'you know what it means, the name of that perfume?"

"Dangerous bait, dangerous allure."

"Yes. Rather apt."

"Come on. I'll buy you a coffee or a drink or something."

"I can't. I have to go. Get me a taxi."

He hadn't much liked being commanded but he hailed a taxi and gave the driver some address in the City she'd told him. While he was holding the door open for her, holding it rather ironically because she took so much for granted, took and tempted and withdrew, she almost floored him with a farewell remark thrown casually over her shoulder.

"Tomorrow, seven, New Quebec Street. O.K.?"

Certainly it was O.K. It was fantastic, also absurd. The taxi moved off, lost itself in the traffic. His hand smelt of *Amorce dangereuse*. Tomorrow, seven, New Quebec Street. He didn't know where New Quebec Street was but he'd find it and he'd be there. An adventure wouldn't do him any harm.

Had he really thought of it like that before it had begun, as an adventure? He remembered that he had and also that it would very likely come to nothing. Arrangements like that which gave the parties thirty hours to think in so often came to nothing . . . But that was how it had happened. Jeff had pinched the last of his paper and, godlike, sent him to Bond Street and to her. Jeff had ruined him, kind Jeff who wouldn't hurt a fly. By rights then, Jeff ought to save him, though no one, of course, could do that except himself.

For he had been ruined. The ream had been started on but only about a hundred of the sheets used up. How can you complete a novel whose purpose is to explore the intricacies of love as you know them when halfway through you find your whole conception has been wrong? When you find that the idea of love on which you based it is vapid and false because you've discovered its true meaning?

Dreaming of her, thinking about her, all night, he was purged of her by the morning. But he knew this wasn't a full catharsis. Possessing him again, his succubus would come to him again in the day and the next night.

A strong furious gale howled about the hovel. No post had come for days. Pushing her firmly out of a mind that felt excoriated, he began worrying about his royalty statement. Why hadn't it come? The last one had arrived early in November, stating the income he'd made up to the previous June, and he'd had the cheque by the end of the month. By now, well by now, he ought to have had the statement for his earnings from June till December. *Maybe there wasn't anything to come.* In the days when the cheques had been for several hundreds he'd never considered whether they'd bother to tell him if there wasn't any money to pay out. Perhaps they didn't. Perhaps their accountants or cashiers or whatever just went heartlessly through a list of names and when they came to him, said, "Oh, Graham Lanceton? Nothing for him. We can forget him."

He hunted out the November statement which he kept in a strongbox in the spare bedroom. There was a phone number on the top of it, the number of their accounts department which was somewhere out in Surrey, miles from the London office. Gray knew that any responsible practical author would simply dial that number, ask to speak to someone in authority and enquire what the hell had happened to his money. He wasn't keen on doing this. He didn't feel he could take, at this period of his life, after the night he'd spent, the brusque voice of some accountant living on a safe three thousand a year telling him his coffers were empty. What he'd do, he decided, was wait one more week and if it still hadn't come he'd phone Peter Marshall. Peter was his own editor and a very nice bloke who'd been charming and hospitable when *The Wine of Astonishment* was born into a waiting world and still charming and kind, though wistful, when it was clear *The Wine of Astonishment* was to have no siblings. Of course, he'd ask if Gray was writing anything and remind him they had the first option on any full-length work of fiction he might produce, but he wouldn't nag or be unpleasant. He'd promise very kindly and reassuringly to look into the matter for him and maybe ask him to lunch.

This decision made, he examined his larder. It was obvious that even he couldn't exist until the end of the month on two cans of mincemeat, a packet of raspberry jelly, and the rock-hard end of a Vienna loaf. Money must be acquired. He thought vaguely of touching Francis (fairly hopeless), of the Social Security (if he was going to do that he'd pack up and do it in London), of selling his watch to the shop near the Abbey which was already in possession of his lighter. He didn't want to part with that watch. The only thing would be to use Honoré's money or part of it. The sheer awfulness of using money sent to one for the reaching of one's mother's deathbed chilled him, but he told himself not to be stupid. Presumably, even Honoré wouldn't want him to starve.

It had begun to rain, was now pouring with rain. He put on Mal's oilskins which hung in the cellar and trudged off through the rain to the bank. There he drew out ten pounds which he meant to spend very sparingly indeed, reducing himself if necessary to a diet of milk, bread, and cheese till the cheque came. He had stuffed the money into a pocket of the oilskins and when he fished in it for a pound he brought out with it a crumpled sheet of paper. Reading it, Gray could hardly believe his eyes. It was nearly six months since he'd worn these oilskins—generally he stayed in when it rained—and he must have shoved the letter from his publishers' contracts manager into this pocket sometime in December. It was dated just before Christmas—Oh, Drusilla, that Christmas!—and it informed him that the Yugoslavian serial rights of *The Wine of Astonishment* had been sold for fifty pounds. A measly sum, but money. He must be going to get a cheque, they hadn't forgotten him. Right, he wasn't going to stint himself. He bought fresh meat, frozen vegetables, bread, real butter, and forty cigarettes, one of which he lit as soon as he was outside the shop.

It made him feel a bit faint. Apart from the one he'd had off Isabel, it was the first he'd smoked since the autumn when he'd always helped himself out of her packets of king-sized.

"I'll have to give it up," he'd said then. "It gets on my conscience, Tiny keeping me in fags, because that's what it amounts to."

"It needn't be that way."

"Don't start. Let's have one day of rest."

"You mentioned him. You brought Tiny up."

There had been no talk of Tiny that first time, no ridiculous diminutive bandied between them, only the hint of a husband somewhere in the background.

"Mrs. Harvey Janus? My God, if I were Mr. Harvey Janus I wouldn't be too happy about this, but since I'm not . . ."

Waiting for her in New Quebec Street, in the complex that lies behind Marble Arch, he hadn't even known her name. She was late and he'd begun to think she wasn't coming. The taxi drew up at twenty past seven when he was on the point of giving up, of realising that it wasn't any use wondering where he was going to take her, whether they were going to walk about or go into a pub or what. A hand was thrust out of the window, beckoning him. She sat in the middle of the seat, dressed in white trousers, a fur jacket, a huge black hat and huge black sunglasses. Sunglasses in January . . .

"Hi. Get in."

He looked at the driver who was staring deadpan in front of him.

"Come on, get in." She tapped on the glass. "The Oranmore Hotel, Sussex Gardens. You don't know it? Can't say I'm surprised. Keep going down Sussex Gardens, it's nearly halfway down on the right."

To say he was flabbergasted was an understatement. He got in, raising his eyebrows at her, and then closed the glass panel between them and the driver. "You might put me in the picture."

"Oh, isn't the picture clear? There's an old girl and her husband keep this place. You just register when we get there, and she'll say you want to pay now, don't you, in case you're leaving early in the morning."

"Well, well." He couldn't get over the speed of it, the lack of preamble. "We don't have to leave too early in the morning, do we?"

"We have to leave at nine thirty tonight, ducky. Just two hours we've got. She'll tell us to leave the key on the dressing table when we go. For God's sake, you don't know much about it, do you?"

"My women usually have flats or rooms."

"Well, I'm a married lady and just for your information I'm supposed to be at my yoga class." She giggled and in that giggle he heard a note of childlike triumph. "It's not everyone I'd sacrifice my yoga class for."

"I'll do my best to make it worth your while."

The Oranmore turned out to be an early nineteenth century house that had probably once been a brothel. It had its name in blue neon over the front door, but both the o's were blacked out.

He registered as Mr. and Mrs. Browne—not so much because the name is common as through association with the title of a peerage —and was given a key for number three. The old woman behaved exactly as had been predicted.

On the stairs Gray said, "Do you have a first name, Mrs. Browne?"

"It's Drusilla," she said.

He unlocked the door. The room was small with twin beds, Junk City furniture, a washbasin, a gas ring. Drusilla pulled down the window blind.

"Drusilla what?" he said, going up to her, putting his hands on her waist. It was a very narrow fragile waist and when he touched it she thrust her pelvis forward. "Drusilla what?"

"Janus. Mrs. Harvey Janus."

"My God, if I were Mr. Harvey Janus I shouldn't be too happy about this, but since I'm not . . ." He unfastened the fur jacket. Underneath it she was naked. He had expected that somehow. Already he was beginning to assess her, the kind of things, daring, provocative, direct, she would do. But he gasped just the same and stepped back, looking at her.

She began to laugh. She took off her hat, the knot of pearl strings from her neck, the jacket, sure, he thought, that she had the situation under control, that it was going to be her way. But he'd had enough of her running things.

"Shut up," he said. He picked her up, lifting her bodily, and she stopped laughing, but her lips remained parted and her moonstone eyes grew very wide. "That's better. Two hours, I think you said?"

She had hardly spoken again for those two hours. That time she hadn't told him anything about herself, hadn't asked his name till they were downstairs again, passing the old woman who, playing her part, had wished them a pleasant evening and reminded them not to forget their key. He took her to the tube at Marble Arch and at the entrance, between the newspaper vendors, she said, "Next Thursday? Same time? Same place?"

"Kiss?"

"You've got an oral fixation," she said but she put up her lips which were thin, delicate, unpainted.

He'd bought a packet of cigarettes, lit one and begun to walk

all the way back to Notting Hill. How had that cigarette tasted?
He couldn't remember. The one he was inhaling on now was
ash-flavoured, a hot rasping smoke. He threw it away among the
bracken, half hoping it would start a fire and the whole of lonely
silent Pocket Lane go up in flames.

That day he hadn't even seen the milkman and he didn't see
anyone else to talk to throughout the weekend. No trippers, no
picnickers, penetrated so far down the lane. Only old Mr. Tringham passed the hovel, taking his Saturday-evening walk, apparently his only walk of the week. Gray saw him from the window,
strolling slowly, reading from a small black book as he walked, but
he didn't lift his head or glance to either side of him.

The phone, still off its hook, hung dumb.

CHAPTER 5

In the middle of the week he got the final demand from the Gas Board and, by the same post, a card from Mal: *Coming home August. Not to worry. We can share the hovel till you find another place.* Mal wouldn't like it if he came back to find they'd cut off the gas, which they'd certainly do if the bill wasn't paid by the weekend. No royalty statement had arrived.

Friday morning and as bitterly cold as November. He'd saved one cigarette and he lit it as he dialled his publishers' London number.

"Mr. Marshall is out for the day," said the girl they'd put him on to. "Can I help?"

"Not really. I'll phone him on Monday."

"Mr. Marshall starts his holiday on Monday, Mr. Lanceton."

That, then, was that. For the rest of the day he debated whether to phone the Surrey department but by half-past five he still hadn't done so and then it was too late. He decided to write to them instead, a good idea which he couldn't understand not having thought of before. When he'd finished the letter and its carbon copy, he sat with his fingers resting on the typewriter keys, thinking about the last time he'd used the machine. The ribbon was nearly worn clean. He'd worn the ribbon out writing those letters to Tiny. The absurdity, the grotesquerie, of that business made him wince. How had he ever been such a fool as to let her persuade him so far, to type those dreadful letters with her standing over him? He'd better make sure he remembered that next time he was tempted into phoning her.

The phone was on its hook but it had a passive look as if it were asleep. It hadn't made a sound since it had opened its mouth more than a week ago to let Francis speak through it, and he hadn't again contemplated ringing that Loughton number. He took his letter and stuck it on the hall window sill. Tomorrow he'd buy a stamp for it.

Saturday was bath day. Until he came to the hovel he'd hardly ever passed a day without a bath. Now he understood why the poor smell and he saw how insensitive are those bathroom owners who won't sympathise with the dirty because washing is free and soap cheap. When you wanted a bath at the hovel you had to heat water up in two saucepans and a bucket and then you didn't get enough hot to cover your knees. Back in the days when he was Drusilla's lover he went through this ritual quite often or stood up at the sink and washed himself all over in cold water. You needed an incentive to do that. After the parting there wasn't much incentive. The milkman never got very close to him and he was past caring what the librarian thought, so these days he had a bath on Saturday and washed his hair in the bath. Then he used the same water to wash his jeans and T-shirt.

All the week he used the bath as a repository for dirty sheets, chucking them on to the floor as a sort of absorbent mat when he was actually in the water. He hadn't been to the launderette for ages and they were getting mildewed. He washed his hair and was just rinsing it, dipping it into the scummy water, when the phone belched out its warning click. Ten seconds later it began to ring. It couldn't be Drusilla, who went shopping with Tiny on Saturdays, so he let it ring till he was out of the bath and wrapped in a grey towel.

Cursing, leaving footprints on the stone hall floor, he went into the "lounge" and picked up the phone. Honoré.

"I disarrange you, I think, my son."

For once, his choice of a word was apt. Gray gathered the damp folds around him, forgetting to talk French in the slight anxiety the call had caused.

"How's Mother?"

"That is for why I call. Mother goes better now so I say, I call to Gray-arm and give him these good news so he is no more unquiet."

Wants his money back, more like, thought Gray. "*Que vous êtes gentil, Honoré. Entendez, votre argent est arrivé dans la banque. Il paraît que je n'en aurai besoin, mais . . .*"

Trust Honoré to interrupt before he'd reached the point of asking whether he could keep the money a little longer.

"Like you say, Gray-arm, you need my money no more and old Honoré know you so well." Gray could see the brown finger wagging, the avaricious knowing smile. "Ah, so well! Better for you and me you send him back, hein? Before you spend him for wine and women."

"This call," said Gray, whose French wasn't adequate for what he wanted to say, "is going to cost you a lot."

"Very sure, so I say goodbye. You send him back today and I get you again if Mummy go less good."

"Right, but don't phone next weekend as I'll be at Francis Croy's place. *Vous comprenez?*"

Honoré said he understood very well and rang off. Gray ran the water out of the bath. It was evident his mother wasn't dying and the money wasn't going to be needed for any trip to France, but it was absurd Honoré wanting it back at once. What difference could it make to him whether he got it now or in, say, a fortnight? Didn't he own his own house and car, all bought out of Gray's father's life assurance? Now he knew his mother wasn't dying, Gray allowed himself to dwell on a usually forbidden subject— her will. Under that, he and Honoré were to have equal shares. When she died . . . No, he'd let himself sink into enough deep dishonour without that. She wasn't going to die for years and when she did he'd have a flat of his own in London and a string of successful novels behind him.

Because it had begun to rain, he draped his wet clothes over a line he put up in the "lounge" and read *Anthony Absolute* dejectedly till the milkman came. The lane had turned bright yellow in the wet, the colour of gamboge in a paintbox, and the wheels of the can were plastered with it.

"Lovely weather for ducks. Pity we're not ducks."

Gray said savagely, "God, how I hate this place."

"Don't be like that, Mr. L. There's some as likes it."

"Where do you live?"

"Walthamstow," said the milkman stoically.

"I wish I lived in Walthamstow. Beats me how anyone can live out here from choice."

"The Forest's very desirable residentially like. Some of them big houses Loughton way are fetching prices you wouldn't believe. Real high-class suburbia, they are."

"Christ," said Gray feelingly. He didn't like to see the milkman look so bewildered and crestfallen, and to know he'd been the cause of it. But his words had gone in like a knife teasing an already open wound.

"Where do you live?" he'd said, drawing one finger down the smooth white body, white as lily petals, blue-veined. "I don't know anything about you."

"Loughton."

"Where's that, for God's sake?"

She made a face, turning her shoulder, giggling. "Real high-class suburbia. You keep going forever down the Central Line."

"D'you like that?"

"I have to live where Tiny lives, don't I?"

"*Tiny?*"

"It's just a nickname, everyone calls him that." She put up her arms, holding him, saying, "I like you a lot, Mr. Browne. Let's keep this going a bit longer, shall we?"

"Not in this dump. Can't I come to your suburb?"

"And have all my neighbours dropping hints to Tiny at bridge parties?"

"Then you'll have to come to Tranmere Villas. Will you mind other people being in the flat?"

"You know," she said, "I think I'll like it."

His eyebrows went up. "That doesn't quite go with the Loughton housewife bit."

"Damn you, I married him when I was eighteen, that's six years ago. I didn't know then. I didn't know a thing."

"You don't have to stay with him."

"I have to stay," she said. "God, who asked you to criticise my life style, Mr. Justice Browne? That's not what I miss my yoga class for. That's not what I strip off for. If you don't want it I'll soon find someone who does."

Toughness, sophistication, hung on her like a call girl's see-through dress on an ingenue. For that's what she was, an ingenue, a green girl, a late starter and he was only her second lover. She didn't admit she knew the Oranmore because she'd been there with her first, or New Quebec Street because she'd once bought a vase in the pottery shop. She didn't admit it but he was a writer and he could tell. He could tell she got that smart wisecracking talk of hers out of books, bought her Harrods clothes because she'd seen them advertised in magazines at the hairdresser's, her hard brittle manner out of films seen at Essex Odeons. He wanted to find the little girl that existed somewhere underneath it all and she wanted equally hard to stop him knowing the little girl was there.

When he met her at the station he knew at once she'd never been to Notting Hill before. If he hadn't stopped her she'd have crossed the street to the Campden Hill side. No one else seeing her would have guessed the underlying naivety from her appearance, the long purple dress, the silver chains, the purple paint on her mouth, for her face was made up that night. He took her to the flat and it was he, not she, who was put off by the bedroom door being accidentally opened and as quickly closed again. So he took her for a walk up through the drab, exotic, decaying streets of North Kensington, into little pubs with red plush and gilded saloon bars. They saw a sad skeletal boy giving himself a fix in a telephone box. She didn't find it sad; her eyes were greedy for what she called life and she made out so well that he almost forgot how innocent she was.

"That cinema," he said, "they smoke in there. The air hangs blue with it."

"They what? Everyone smokes in cinemas."

"I meant pot, Drusilla."

The little girl turned on him furiously. "Damn you! I can't help not knowing. I want to know. I want to be free to know things and you—you bloody laugh at me. I want to go home."

And then he had really laughed at her, poor little child in adult's clothes, who wanted both to be free and to be safe at home; little sheltered girl, protected all her life. Tantalised by innocence that should have, but didn't, go hand in hand with prudery, thinking only of the delight she gave him, he hadn't considered the full significance of a child in a grown-up body. He hadn't thought then what it must mean—to have an adult's subtlety, command of language and sensual capacity without an adult's humanity.

"I didn't know you owned a house," Gray said when Mal dropped in at Tranmere Villas one night, a fortnight before he left for Japan.

"It's just a hovel, no hot water, no mod cons. I had a Premium Bond come up about five years ago and someone said property was the thing, so I bought this place. I go to it sometimes at weekends."

"Where is it, for God's sake?"

"Epping Forest, near Waltham Abbey. I was born near there. I mention it because I was wondering if you'd like to take it on while I'm away."

"Me? I'm a Londoner. It's not my scene."

"It's just the place for you to write your masterpiece. Isolated, dead quiet. I wouldn't want rent. But I do want someone to see it doesn't fall into rack and ruin."

"Sorry. You've come to the wrong shop."

"Maybe the right shop," said Mal, "would be an estate agent's. I'd better try and sell it. I'll get hold of an agent in Enfield or Loughton."

"*Loughton?*"

"It's four miles from there. D'you know it?"

"In a sort of way I do."

So he'd agreed to take care of the hovel because it was only four miles from Loughton . . .

"A funny sort of lane east of Waltham Abbey?" said Drusilla when he told her.

" 'The beds i' the East are soft.' "

"Beds, floor, stairs, kitchen table, it's all the same to me, ducky. I expect I could pop over quite often."

The beds were no longer soft. There is no bed so hard as the one deserted by one's lover. For her sake he had come here and now she was gone there was no longer anything to keep him but poverty.

He paid the gas bill, went to the library (*The Sun Is My Un-*

doing, The Green Hat, King Solomon's Mines) but forgot to buy a stamp. Well, he'd buy one on Monday, post the letter, and as soon as the money came—as soon as there was a definite prospect of the money—he'd shake the dust of this place off his feet for ever.

Mr. Tringham went by at six thirty, reading his book. He too could become like that one day, Gray thought, a hermit who has grown to love his solitude and who jealously preserves it. He must get away.

CHAPTER 6

He finally posted the letter on Wednesday. By that time he had just seven pounds of Honoré's money left and he'd have to save that for incidental expenses in London. There were bound to be plenty. Francis would expect a bottle and some cigarettes and probably a meal out. By Monday he'd be skint but by Monday the statement and the cheque would have arrived. He'd allow himself a week at the hovel to clean it up a bit—get some of those stains off the bedroom haircord, for instance—and then he'd ask Jeff to cart his stuff away the following weekend. Francis, if handled right, might just possibly agree to put him up for a week or two. A happier state of affairs, of course, would be to meet some girl at the party who had a room of her own and who liked him enough to shack up with him. He'd have to like her enough too and that would be the trouble. Drusilla had spoilt other women for him.

"After me," she'd said, "other women'll be like cold mutton."

"You got that out of a book. Sounds like Maugham."

"So what? It's true."

"Maybe. And what will other blokes be like for you?"

"You scared I might go back to Ian?"

Ian was his predecessor, a sportsman, tennis coach or something, the man who'd introduced her to the amenities of the Oranmore. Gray couldn't play her game of pretending not to care. He was beginning to care quite a lot.

"Yes, I'm scared of losing you, Dru."

At first she'd scoffed at the hovel. She'd gone all over it, laughing incredulously, amazed that there was no bathroom, no indoor loo. But he'd let her know it wasn't the thing these days to be snobbish about material things. She learned fast and soon she was as slapdash about the place as he, using saucers for ashtrays and putting her teacup on the floor.

"Who cleans your place?" he'd asked.

"A woman comes in every day," she said, but still he didn't understand quite how rich she was.

The first time she came to the hovel he walked back down the lane with her to where she'd left her car. A Mini, he expected it to be, and when he saw the E-type, he said, "Come off it. You're joking."

"Am I? Look, the key fits."

"Who does it really belong to? Tiny?"

"It's mine. Tiny gave it me for my last birthday."

"God, he must be rolling in it. What does he do?"

"Property," she said. "Directorships. He's got his finger in a lot of very lucrative pies."

And then he knew she'd been telling the truth when she said her dress came from Dior, that the rings she took off when they made love were platinum and diamonds. Tiny wasn't just well-off, making ends meet comfortably on five thousand a year. He was rich by anyone's standards, what even rich people call rich. But it had never occurred to Gray to try and get his hands on some of it. In fact, he avoided the subject of her wealth, careful not to let any of it rub off on him via her. It seemed ugly that he who had stolen—at least, temporarily—Tiny's wife, should be enriched even in a small way by Tiny's money.

She'd read his book and liked it but she never nagged him about writing anything else. That was one of the things he liked about her. She wasn't moralistic. No "You ought to work, think of your future, settle down," from her. Preaching had no place in her nature. She was a hedonist, enjoying herself, taking from whoever was prepared to give, but giving of herself amply in return. It was because she gave so much, all her body, all her thoughts, reserving nothing, confessing to him with a child's simplicity every need and emotion which most girls would have kept hidden, that it became not a matter of liking her any more, but of love. He knew he was in love with her when one day she didn't phone and he spent the day thinking she was dead or gone back to Ian, the night lying wakeful until the next day she did phone and the world was transformed for him.

She'd come to him in the mornings, in the afternoons, but Thursday had been their evening together. Thursday was the one evening she could be sure of being free of Tiny, and no Thursday ever passed without his thinking of her alone, perhaps taking her own receiver off as he was doing now. He stood looking at the deadened instrument for some time, just standing there and looking at it. Alexander Graham Bell had a lot to answer for. There was something sinister, frightening, dreadful, about a telephone. It seemed to him as if all the magic which in ancient times had manifested itself in divination, in strange communions across land and ocean, in soul-binding spells, conjurations, fetishes that could kill by the power of fright, were now condensed and concentrated into the compact black body of this instrument. A night of sleep might depend on it, days of happiness; its ring could break a life or raise hilarity, wake the near-dead, bring to the tense body utter relaxation. And its power was inescapable. While you possessed one of its allotropes—or it possessed you—you were constantly subject to it, for though you might disarm it as he had just done, it wasn't really gagged. It always retained its ultimate secret weapon, the braying howl, the long-drawn-out crescendo cry of an encaged but still dangerous animal, which was its last resort. Hadn't she once put the howlers on him when, by chance—no leaving the receiver off deliberately in those days—he'd replaced it imperfectly?

"Playing hard to get, lovey? You can't get away from me as easily as that."

But he had got away and into his miserable high-principled freedom, though not easily, not easily—how long would it take before it got easier? He slammed the door shut on the muck and dust and the immobilised phone and went upstairs to look out some gear to wear at Francis's party. His one decent pair of trousers, his one good jacket, were rolled up in the bottom of the bedroom cupboard where he'd slung them after that London weekend with Drusilla. He took out the cream silk shirt, dirty and creased, *Amorce dangereuse* breathing from its creases as he unfolded it. In the darkening bedroom with its low ceiling, rain pattering overhead on the slates, he knelt on the haircord, on the tea stains, and pressed the silk against his face, smelling her smell.

"Shall I wear your shirt to go out in? Do I look good?"

"You look great," he'd said. Fox-gold hair cloaking the cream silk, blood-red fingernails like jewels scattered on it, her naked breasts swelling out the thin, almost transparent stuff. "What am I supposed to wear? Your blouse?"

"I'll buy you another shirt, ducky."

"Not with Tiny's money, you won't."

Tiny had gone on a business trip to Spain. That was how they'd managed the weekend. Until then he'd never had a whole night with her. He'd wanted Cornwall but she'd insisted on London, the Oranmore.

"I want to go to way-out places and do decadent things. I want to explore vice."

"Doriana Gray," he said.

"Damn you, you don't understand. You've been free to do what you like for ten years. I had my father keeping me down and I went straight from him to Tiny. There's always been someone bloody looking after me. I can't go out without publishing where I'm going or making up lies. I'll have to phone Madrid in a minute to keep him quiet. You don't know what it's like never to do *anything.*"

"Darling," he'd said very tenderly, "they're nothing, these things, when you're used to them. They're boring, they're ordinary. Imagine the people who think living in your place and having your clothes and your car and your holidays the acme of sophistication. But to you it's all—ordinary."

She took no notice of him. "I want to go to awful places and smoke pot and see live shows and blue films."

Christ, he'd thought, she was so *young*. That's what he'd thought then, that it was all bravado, and they'd quarrelled because his London wasn't the London she said she wanted; because he wouldn't take her round Soho or to the drag ball she'd seen advertised, but to little cinemas with mid-'30s kitsch décor, Edwardian pubs, the Orangery in Kensington Gardens, the Mercury Theatre, the mewses, and the canal at Little Venice. But she'd enjoyed it, after all, making him laugh with her shrewd comments and her flashes of surprising sensitivity. When the weekend was over and he back at the hovel, he'd missed her with a real aching agony and it wasn't just laziness that made him not wash out the shirt. He kept it unwashed for the scent that imbued it, knowing even then when their affair was a year old and almost at its zenith that the time would come when he'd need objects to evoke memory, objects in which life is petrified, more present (as he'd read somewhere) than in any of its actual moments.

Well, the time had come, the time to remember and the time to wash away memories. He took the clothes downstairs, washed the shirt and went down into the cellar. He hadn't got an electric iron but there was an old flatiron in the cellar, left there by the occupant before Mal.

The cellar steps were steep, leading about fifteen feet into the bowels of the Forest. It was a brick-walled, stone-flagged chamber where he kept his paraffin and where former owners had left a broken bike, an antique sewing machine, ancient suitcases and stacks of damp yellowish newspapers. The iron was among these newspapers along with the thing Gray thought was called a trivet. He took it up to the kitchen and put it on the gas.

Now that he'd made up his mind to leave the hovel, he no longer had to pretend to himself that this kitchen where he'd spent the greater part of two years was less horrible and squalid than it was. In all that time he'd never really cleaned it and the condensation of cooking and gas fumes had run unchecked, unwiped, down the pea-green painted walls. The sink was scored all over with brown cracks and under it was a ganglion of grime-coated pipes, hung with dirty cloths. An unshaded bulb, hanging from the veined and cobwebby ceiling, illuminated the place dully, showing up the cigarette burns and the tea stains on the line. Mal had asked him to see it didn't go to rack and ruin, so it was only fair to Mal to clean it up. Next week he'd have a real spring clean.

It was pitch-dark outside, soundless but for the faint pattering of rain. He got up out of the Windsor chair and spread his velvet trousers on top of the bath cover. He'd never handled the flatiron before, only electric irons with insulated handles. Of course he knew very well you needed a kettle holder or an old sock or something before you got hold of a hot iron bar, but he'd acted instinctively, without thought. The pain was violent, scarlet, roaring. He dropped the iron with a shout, cursing, clutching his burnt hand and falling back into the chair.

When he looked at his hand there was a bright red weal across the palm. And the pain travelled up his wrist, his arm, a pain that was almost a noise in the silence. After a while he got up and held his hand under the cold tap. The shock was so great that it brought tears to his eyes, and when he'd turned off the tap and dried his hand, the tears didn't stop. He began to cry in earnest, abandoning himself to a storm of weeping, sobbing against his folded arms. He knew he wasn't crying because he'd burnt his hand, though that had caused the first tears. Full release had never come to him before, the release of all that pent-up pain. He was crying now for Drusilla, for obsession unconquered, for loneliness and squalor and waste.

His hand was stiff and painful. It felt enormous, a lump of raw flesh hanging from the end of his arm. He hung it outside the bed, the sour sweat-smelling sheets, and lay, tossing and turning, until the birds started their dawn song and pale grey waterish light came through the faded curtains. Then at last he slept, falling at once into a dream of Tiny.

He'd never seen Drusilla's husband and she'd never described him to him. She hadn't needed to. He knew very well what a forty-year-old rich property dealer would look like, a man whose facetious parents or envious school fellows had called Tiny because even as a child he'd been huge and gross. A vast man with thinning black hair, who drank hard, smoked heavily, was vulgar, taciturn, and jealous.

"What does he talk about? What do you do when you're alone together?"

She giggled. "He's a man, isn't he? What d'you think we do?"

"Drusilla, I don't mean that." (Too painful to think of, imagine, then or now). "What have you got in common?"

"We have the neighbours in for drinks. We go shopping on Saturdays. He's got his old mum that we go and see once a week after the shopping, and that's a right drag. As a matter of fact, he collects old coins."

"Oh, *darling!*"

"It's not my bloody fault. He's got his car, it's a red Bentley, and we go out in that to eating places with his dreary middle-aged mates."

Tiny was in that car, the red Bentley he'd never seen, when he dreamed about him. He was standing by the side of the road, one of the Forest roads that converge at the Wake Arms, when the Bentley came up the A.11. Tiny was at the wheel. He knew it was Tiny, the man in the car was so big and so flashily dressed. Besides, one does know these things in dreams. The car screamed to a slower speed, slower than the eighty it had been doing, and then Tiny roared on but not round the roundabout. He careered over the grass mound in the middle of it, the car leaping and jerking until it bounded into the air and crashed, bursting into flames among the scattering, hooting traffic that was coming the other way.

Gray crept forward along with the other people who crowded round the burning car. The car was burning, Tiny was burning, a living torch. But he was still conscious, still aware. He lifted his charred, flame-licked face and shouted at Gray, "Murderer! Murderer!"

Gray tried to stop him, thrusting his hand over that red-hot mouth that was a glowing cinder now, crushing the words away, plunging his fingers into a cavern of fire. He woke up, thrashing about on the bed, staring at his hand which bore on its palm the mark of Tiny's burning lips.

CHAPTER 7

A long oval blister crossed his palm from forefinger to wrist. He lay in bed most of Thursday, sleeping intermittently, waking to stare obsessively at his injured hand. His hand was branded, and it seemed to him, because of that vivid terrible dream, that the burn was Tiny's way of punishing him.

When at last he got up it was early evening, Thursday evening. He took the phone receiver off carefully, holding it between thumb and forefinger. In the cloudy spotted mirror his face looked cadaverous, the eye sockets like hollow bruises. A line from some half-forgotten play, Shakespeare probably, came to him and, staring at his face and the burnt hand which had gone up to shield it, he whispered it aloud, Let me know my trespass by its own visage. Let me know my trespass . . . He had trespassed against Tiny, against her perhaps, most violently against himself.

He slept heavily that night, sliding from dream to dream without any return to consciousness, and in the morning his hand was still throbbing, pulsating like an overtaxed heart. The bandage he made from strips torn off a sheet didn't help much, and he had to make tea and iron the shirt and trousers with his left hand. There was a small hole in the trousers just below the right knee, a hole Drusilla had made, brushing against him with her cigarette, but it would just have to stay there as darning was now beyond him.

"I can't mend it," she'd said. "I wouldn't know how."

"What d'you do when your own things need mending?"

"Throw them away. Do I look as if I wore mended clothes?"

"I can't throw them away, Dru. I can't afford to."

She did something very rare with her. She kissed him. She brought her delicate lips that really were like the petals of some flower, an orchid perhaps, up to his face and kissed him on the corner of his mouth. It was a very tender gesture, and something in him, something that had been mocked by her too often to be anything but wary at tenderness, made him say, "Careful, Drusilla, you'll be loving me next."

"Damn you! What do I care if you bloody starve? I'd give you money, only you won't take it."

"Not Tiny's, I won't."

The trousers had never been mended and nor had his watch which had stopped the same week and refused to go again. On the Thursday night when they'd made love in the hovel, had walked in the forest in the moonlight and at last were sitting in the "lounge" in front of the fire they'd made, she gave him a new watch, the one he now wore, the one he'd never sell no matter what.

"It's beautiful and I love you, but I can't take it."

"Tiny didn't pay for it. My dad gave me a cheque for my birthday."

"Coals to Newcastle, that must have been."

"Maybe, but these coals aren't tainted. Don't you like it?"

"I love it. It makes me feel like a kept man but I love it."

Moonstone eyes, the colour of transparent cloud through which the blue sky shows; white skin, blue-veined at the temples; hair like the pale hot flames that warmed them.

"I'd like you to be a kept man. I'd like Tiny to die so that we could have all that loot for us."

"What, marry me, d'you mean?" The thought had never before crossed his mind.

"To hell with marriage! Don't talk about it." She shuddered, speaking of marriage as some people speak of cancer. "You don't want to get married, do you?"

"I'd like to live with you, Dru, be with you all the time. Marriage or not, I shouldn't mind."

"The house alone'd fetch a fortune. He's got hundreds of thousands in the bank and shares and whatever. Be nice if he had a coronary, wouldn't it?"

"Not for him," he said.

The watch she'd given him just ten months before the end of it all told him now it was twelve noon. But it was Friday so the milkman wouldn't get there till nearly three. He went down into

Waltham Abbey, returned the library books but took out no fresh ones, and at the bank drew out seven pounds, thus emptying his account. On the way back he met the milkman who gave him a lift to the hovel on his van.

"Going to be a scorcher tomorrow, I reckon," said the milkman. "If you're out when I come I'll pop the milk in the shade, shall I?"

"I shan't want any milk till Monday, thanks. Come to think of it, I shan't want any more milk ever. I'm moving out next week." That would spur his going. He could always buy milk when he went into Waltham Abbey for the few days that remained to him of next week. "Getting out of here for good," he said.

The milkman looked quite upset. "Well, it'll make my work lighter. I shan't have to come all the way down here. But I'll miss you, Mr. L. No matter how low I felt, I could always count on you to cheer me up."

One of the Pagliacci, Gray thought, one of the sad clowns. All the time he'd been so wretched the milkman had seen him as a lighthearted joker. He'd have liked to have achieved just one last mild wisecrack—very little wit was ever needed—but he couldn't manage it. "Yes, well, we've had a good laugh, haven't we, one way and another?"

"It's what makes the world go round," said the milkman. "Er—you won't mind me pointing out you owe me forty-two pee?"

Gray paid him.

"When are you going?"

"Tomorrow, but I'll be back again for a few days."

The milkman gave him his change and then, unexpectedly, held out his hand. Gray had to take it and have his own blistered hand shaken agonisingly. "See you, then."

"See you," said Gray, though the chances were he'd never see the milkman again.

He had nothing to read and his burnt hand kept him from starting on the spring clean. Instead, he passed the rest of that hot day sorting through his papers, some of which were in the strongbox, the rest in an untidy heap on top of the disused range. It wasn't a task calculated to cheer him. Among the pile on the range, he found four old royalty statements, each one showing a smaller amount than its predecessor, a demand for back tax he hadn't paid, and—most troubling of all—a dozen drafts of, or attempts at, letters to Tiny.

Rereading them made him feel a little sick. They were only pieces of paper, creased, soiled, thumb-marked, some bearing no more than two or three lines of typed words, but the motive behind them had been destructive. They had been designed to lure a man to that holocaust, realised, as it happened, only in dreams of fire.

Each one was dated, and the whole series spanned a period from June to December. Although he'd never really intended that any one of them should be sent, although he'd typed them only to humour her, he felt that he was looking at a side of himself which he didn't know at all, at a cruel and subtle alter ego which lay buried deep under the layers of idleness, talent, humanity, and saneness, but was nevertheless real. Why hadn't he burned them long ago? At any rate, he'd burn them now.

In a space that was clear of nettles down by the back fence he made a little fire and fed it with the letters. A thin spire of smoke, sequinned with red sparks, rose into the night air. It was all over and dead in five minutes.

He'd never before seen the Forest in its golden cloak of morning mist, it was so rare for him to be up this early. The squirrel was sitting where the fire had been.

"You can move in if you like," Gray said. "Be my guest. You can keep your nuts in the cellar."

He bathed and put on a T-shirt and the velvet trousers, hoping the hole didn't show. The silk shirt was to be saved for Sunday night and he packed it into his bag along with his toothbrush and a sweater. There was no point in going into the "lounge" before he left or changing the filthy sheets, but he washed the dishes with his left hand and left them to drain. By nine he was on his way to the station at Waltham Cross.

The tube didn't come out this way. You had to catch a train that went from Harlow (or somewhere equally remote) to Liverpool Street. The powers that be, he often thought, had been singularly narrow in their attitude to the travel requirements of the residents of Pocket Lane and its environs. It was possible to go to London or Enfield or places no one would want to go to in Hertfordshire, extremely difficult to get to Loughton or anywhere in that direction except by car or on foot. The only time he'd been to Loughton he'd walked to the Wake Arms and caught the 20 bus that came from Epping.

"I can't think why you want to see my place," she'd said, "but you can if you want. You could come on Thursday evening. Just this once though, mind. If the neighbours see you I'll say you came selling encyclopaedias. They think I have it off with the tradesmen, anyway."

"I hope you'll have it off with this tradesman."

"Well, you know me," she said.

Did he? The Thursday they'd chosen was in early spring when the trees of the Forest weren't yet in leaf but hazed all over with the golden-brown of their buds, when the flowers were on the blackthorn but the holly berries still scarlet. He caught the bus to one of the fringe-of-the-forest ponds, a water-filled gravel pit, overlooked by the large houses that sprang up in this district on every bit of land they'd let you build on. Everywhere there were trees, so that in summer the houses would seem to stand in the Forest itself. It would be, he'd decided, in such a one that she lived, a four-bedroomed Tudor-style villa.

She'd drawn him a little plan and told him which way to go. The sun had gone but it would be an hour yet before it was dark. He walked along a road on one side of which open green land, dotted with bushes, fell away into a valley. Beyond this valley the Forest rose in blue-black waves. On the other side were old cottages of weatherboard and slate like the hovel, new houses, a pub. They called the district he was approaching, the part where she lived, Little Cornwall, because it was exceptionally hilly and from its hills, she'd said, you could look down into Loughton which lay in a basin below, and then on and on over Metropolitan Essex, over the "nice" suburbs, the distant docks, and see sometimes the light shining on the Thames.

It was too dark for that by the time he'd reached the top of the hill. Lights were coming out everywhere over the blue spread of land. He turned off along Wintry Hill and found himself in a lane—gates in high fences, trees overhanging, long drives disappearing into shrubberies and leading to distant hidden houses.

The Forest hung behind them, densely black against a primrose sky. And he felt that this was very different from the area around the pond. This was grandeur, magnificence and, in a way, awesome. Her house (Tiny's house) was called Combe Park, a name which she'd got haughty and self-conscious about when she'd mentioned it and which he'd laughed at as absurdly pretentious.

But it wasn't pretentious. He came to the end of the lane to face wrought-iron gates which stood open. The name COMBE PARK was lettered on these gates and he saw at once that it hadn't been bestowed with the intention to impress on some detached three-bedroomed affair. The grounds were enormous, comprising lawns and flowerbeds and an orchard which was a mass of daffodils, a pond as large as a small lake and ringed with rockeries on which cypresses, twice as tall as a man, were dwarfed by overhanging willows and cedars. The neighbours would have needed periscopes as well as binoculars to see the house through those tree screens. Not that the house itself wasn't large. He saw an enormous box, flat-roofed and balconied, part of white stucco, part cedar-boarded, with a kind of glass sun lounge on its roof and a York stone terrace spreading away from front door and plate-glass picture windows. The terrace was set about with white metal furniture and evergreens in marble urns.

At first he'd thought it couldn't be hers, that he couldn't know (let alone, love) anyone that affluent. But this was Combe Park all right. The triple (quadruple? quintuple?) garage, a large house in itself, had its doors wide open and inside he could see the E-type, reduced to Mini scale by the vastness of its shelter. There was no red Bentley to keep it company but, just the same, he didn't move from the position he'd taken up and in which he felt frozen outside the gate. He didn't want to go in, he wasn't going in. He forgot then that it was he who'd invited himself, who'd insisted, and thought only of his poverty, her wealth, and that if he set foot on that drive and began to walk up it under her eye, he'd feel like the village boy sent for by the squire's lady. And he might start getting greedy too. He might start thinking of that coronary she'd wished on Tiny.

So he'd walked back to the bus stop, caught the bus after half an hour's wait, walked back to Pocket Lane, and before he'd been in the house five minutes the phone started.

"Damn you! I saw you at the gate and I came down to open the door and you'd bloody gone. Were you scared?"

"Only of your money, Drusilla."

"God," she'd said, drawling then, the little girl voice submerged in the lady-who-picks-up-men voice. "It could all be yours if he had a heart attack or a car crash. Yours and mine. Wouldn't that be super?"

"That's just pointless fantasy," he'd said.

He got on at Liverpool Street tube station and out at Bayswater. Queensway, very lively with its clothes shops and fruit shops, Whiteley's cupola, the interesting trendy people, cheered him up. And the weather was perfect, the bright blue sky giving Porchester Hall an almost classical look to his London-starved eyes.

Francis lived in one of those old streets of Victorian houses, each one separate and each one different, each in its garden of very old London shrubs and town flowers that seem faded to pale pinks and golds by dust and hard light, which lie to the north of Westbourne Grove. Francis's flat was the conservatory of one of these houses, a red and blue crystal palace partitioned off into two rooms with bathroom and kitchen added.

He opened the crimson glass door to Gray and said, "Hallo, you're late. Just as well I don't have to meet my aunt after all. We can get on with moving the furniture. This is Charmian."

Gray said, "Hi," and wished he hadn't because Hi was what he said to Drusilla. Charmian, who in any case, was probably booked for Francis, wasn't the girl to rid him of Drusilla, being plump, snub-nosed, and ungainly. She had a lot of jolly fair curls and she wore a very short skirt which showed her fat thighs. While she looked on, sitting cross-legged on a windowsill and eating a banana, Gray helped Francis move the enormous Victorian sideboard and tallboy from the living room into the bedroom, and moved beds out to make divans for exhausted, lecherous or stoned guests. His hand was thickly bandaged but it throbbed, sending shafts of pain up his arm.

Francis said discouragingly, "I tried to phone you to tell you not to bother to come till tomorrow but your line's always engaged. I suppose you leave the receiver off. What are you scared of? Your creditors?"

Charmian laughed shrilly. The receiver was still off, Gray realised. It had been off since Thursday evening.

Presently the men arrived to fix up the winking lights. They took hours about it, drinking very inferior tea made by Charmian with tea bags. Gray wondered when they were going to get a meal, as both Francis and the girl had said they were on diets. At last the men went and the three of them went down to the Redan where Francis and Charmian drank orange juice in accordance with their diets and Gray drank beer. It was nearly six o'clock.

"I hope you've got some money on you. I've left mine in my other jacket."

Gray said he had. He thought Francis lucky to possess another jacket. "When you've had that orange juice, maybe you'll go back and fetch it and then we can eat somewhere."

"Well, actually, Charmian and I are dining with some people we don't know very well. I only mention that about our not knowing them to show we can't exactly take a stranger with us."

"Not very well," said Charmian. She had been staring fixedly at Gray for some minutes and now she launched suddenly into a lecture. "I read your book. Francis lent it to me. I think it's terrible your not writing anything else. I mean, not doing any work at all. I know it's nothing to do with me . . ."

"No, it isn't."

"Steady, now," said Francis.

The girl took no notice of either of them. "You live in that dreadful place like a sort of country hippy and you're just not together. You're all spaced out. I mean, you leave your phone off for days and when you're with people half the time you're not, if you know what I mean. You're off on a sort of trip of your own. No one would *believe* you'd written *The Wine of Astonishment*."

Gray shrugged. "I'm going to eat and then I'm going to the pictures," he said. "Have a good time with the people you don't know."

Of course she was quite right, he thought, as he went off on his own to find a cheap Chinese restaurant. It wasn't her business and she was a stupid boring girl, but she was right. He'd have to do something and quick.

The people who sat at the tables around him and something she'd said about a trip were reawakening memories he'd thought London would help to exorcise. He sucked a sugar loaf from the paper-thin china bowl in front of him. It was only a sugar loaf. It wouldn't distort reality any more than he could distort it himself . . .

Drusilla in spring, Drusilla before the letters started—"You know a lot of weird freaky people, don't you?" she'd said. "All that Westbourne Grove-Portobello Road lot?"

"I know some."

"Gray, could you get hold of some LSD?"

He was so unused to hearing it called by those initials that, although decimal coinage had been in for a year and more, he said, "Money? How?"

"Oh, God, I don't mean money. I mean acid. Could you get us some acid?"

CHAPTER 8

First the Classic Cinema in Praed Street where he saw an old Swedish film full of pale Strindbergian people in Grimms Fairy Tale forests, and then, for the night was warm and clear, he walked southwards across Sussex Gardens.

The Oranmore wasn't there any more. Or, rather, it was there but it had been painted glistening white and a new name, this time in veridian neon, stuck up above the portico: THE GRAND EUROPA. Combe Park hadn't been a pretentious name but this was. A large German tourist coach was parked outside, disgorging what looked like the Heidelberg Community Centre ladies' package tour. The ladies, large and tired, all wearing hats, drifted with bewilderment through the front door, driven by brisk polyglot couriers. Gray wondered if the old woman would give them each a key and tell them to leave it on the dressing table because she knew they'd want to leave early in the morning. He felt sorry for the German ladies, told, no doubt, that they'd be staying in the heart of trendy London, in a quaint period hotel within walking distance of Oxford Street and the Park, and then landing up at the Oranmore. It didn't, after all, hold for any of them his own memories of lost splendour.

A young porter came down the steps to help them; behind him a bright young woman. It seemed as if the old people had gone, along with the old name. He turned down the Edgware Road, a great ache inside him, a hungry longing to hear her voice just once more.

The letters slid into a dark curtained recess of his memory. In the light exposed parts, as bright as this blazingly lit street, all the joy she'd brought him seemed to shine. If he could have her without demands, without complications! It was impossible—yet to hear her voice just once?

Suppose he were to phone her now? It was nearly midnight. She'd be in one of the beds in the room she shared with Tiny, the room that overlooked those black waves of forest. Tiny would be there too, asleep possibly; possibly sitting up reading one of those books he was so fond of, memoirs of some tycoon or retired general, and she'd be reading a novel. Although he'd never been in the bedroom, he could see them, the gross bloated man, curly black hair showing at the open neck of red and black silk pyjamas, the slim girl in white frills, her fiery hair loose, and around them all the lush appointments of a rich man's bedroom, white pile rugs, white brocade curtains, Pompadour furniture, ivory and gold. Between them, the white, silent, threatening phone.

He could phone her but not speak to her. That way he'd hear her voice. When she didn't know who was calling, when it wasn't someone to say "Hi" to, she just said "Yes?" with cool indifference. She'd say "Yes?" and when there wasn't any reply, "Who the hell *is* that?" But he couldn't phone her now, not at midnight.

He walked down past the Odeon Cinema to Marble Arch. The last of the queue was going in for the midnight movie. There were still a lot of people about. He knew he was going to have to phone her. It was as if it was too late to go back, though he'd done nothing, taken no decisive step, only thought. He went into Marble Arch tube station and into a phone booth. For two pence he could buy her voice, a word or two, whole sentences if he was lucky and got a bargain. His heart was thudding and his hands were wet with sweat. Suppose someone else answered? Suppose they'd moved? They could be on holiday, taking the first of those two or three annual holidays which in the past had brought him postcards and loneliness. With a sweaty hand he lifted the receiver and placed a finger in the five slot on the dial.

Five-O-eight, then all the four digits including the final nine. He leant against the wall, the receiver cold as ice against his branded palm. I am a little mad, he thought, I'm breaking down . . . They might have gone out with those friends to a roadhouse, they might . . . He heard the whistling peep-peep that told him he was through and, trembling, he pressed in his coin. It fell through the machinery with a hollow crash.

"Yes?"

Not Tiny, not some newcomer, but she. The single mono-syllable was repeated impatiently. "Yes?"

He'd resolved not to speak to her but he needed no resolve. He couldn't speak, though he breathed like one of those men who phone women in the night to frighten them. She wasn't easily frightened.

"Who the hell's that?"

He listened, not as if she were speaking to him—as indeed she wasn't—but as though this were a tape someone was playing to him.

"Listen," she said, "whoever you are, some bloody joker, you've had your kick, you pervert, so just piss off!"

The phone went down with a crack like a gunshot. He lit a cigarette with shaking fingers. Well, he'd had what he wanted, her voice, the last of her to remember. She'd never speak to him again and he'd be able to remember forever her parting words, the positively last appearance of the prima donna—piss off, you pervert. He went back into the street, swaying like a drunk.

It was about ten in the morning when Francis appeared by his bed with an unexpected cup of tea. Francis had slept in the bedroom, Gray on one of the beds that had been moved into the main room where the sun now penetrated in red, blue, and golden rays through the glass and made dancing blobs on the floor.

"I owe you an apology for that carry-on in the pub yesterday. Charmian's a wonderful girl but she is impulsive."

"That's all right."

"I Spoke to Her About It," said Francis rather pompously. "After all, what you'd take from an old mate like me doesn't come too well from someone you've just met. But she's a marvellous girl, isn't she?"

Gray smiled neutrally. "Are you and she . . . ?"

"We aren't yet having a sexual relationship, if that's what you mean. Charmian views these things very seriously. Time will tell, of course. It might be as well for me to consider marriage quite soon."

"Quite soon?" said Gray, alarmed at possible interference with his plans. "You and Charmian mean to marry quite soon?"

"My God, no. It may not even be with Charmian. It's just that I think marriage should be the next big event I plan for in my life."

Gray drank his tea. Now was the moment and he'd better seize it. "Francis, I want to come back to London."

"Of course you do. I've been telling you for ages."

"I'll get paid quite soon and when I do—well, could I come here for a bit while I look for a room?"

"Here? With me?"

"It wouldn't be for more than a month or two."

Francis looked rather sour. "It'll be very inconvenient. I'd have to have help with the rent. This place costs me eighteen a week, you know."

There'd be at least fifty when the cheque came . . . "I'd go halves."

Maybe it was his guilt over the lecture he'd exposed Gray to the night before that made Francis put aside his usual scepticism when his friend mentioned making monetary contributions to anything. "Well, I suppose so," he said ungraciously. "Let's say you'll stay six weeks. When d'you want to come? Charmian and I are going down to Devon to her people tomorrow for a few days. How about next Saturday?"

"Saturday," said Gray, "would suit me fine."

After he'd had a bath—in a proper bathroom with hot water coming out of a tap—he walked over to Tranmere Villas. Jeff was still in bed and it was the tenant of Gray's old room, the room where just once he'd made love to Drusilla, who admitted him to the flat.

"Sally out?" he said when Jeff appeared, sleepy, gloomy, and myopic without his glasses.

"She's left me. Walked out a few weeks back."

"God, I'm sorry." He knew how it felt. "You'd been together a long time."

"Five years. She met this bloke and went off with him to the Isle of Mull."

"I *am* sorry."

Jeff made coffee and they talked about Sally, the bloke, loneliness, the Isle of Mull, a man they'd been at school with who was now Gray's M.P. and then about various people they'd known in the old days, all of whom seemed to have gone off to remote places. Gray told his friend about the move.

"Yes, I could shift your stuff on Saturday. There isn't much of it, is there?"

"Some books, a typewriter, clothes."

"Say midafternoon, then? If you change your plans you can give me a ring. By the way, there's a letter here for you, came about a month back just when Sally went. It looked like a bill so what with Sally and everything, I never got around to sending it on. I know I should have done but I was in a hell of a mess. Thank God, I'm getting myself together again now."

Gray wished he could do the same. He took the envelope, knowing what it was before he opened it. How could he forget so much that was important when he remembered everything that was past and dead and useless? She'd left him and he'd gone to London for Christmas with Francis, resolving then never to go back to the hovel, never to set foot within ten miles of her. And he'd written to his publishers asking them to send the next statement to Tranmere Villas because that was the one address he could be sure of being permanent. How could he have forgotten? Because he'd felt so hopeless and disorientated that he'd drifted back to Pocket Lane, fleeing from the tough members of his tribe like a wounded animal seeking the shelter of its lair?

He slit open the envelope. *The Wine of Astonishment*: Sales, home, £5; 75% sales, French, £3.50; 75% sales, Italian, £6.26. Total, £14.76.

"Since you're not doing anything," said Charmian, "you can give me a hand with the food. We're not having a real lunch, just picking at bits from this lot." "This lot" was a heap of lettuces, tomatoes, plastic wrapped cheese, envelopes of sliced meat and French loaves. "Unless you feel like treating us to a meal."

"Now then, lovey," said Francis.

Gray wasn't annoyed with her. He was too shattered by the royalty statement to feel anything much. On the way to Jeff's he'd bought a bottle of Spanish Chablis for the party and now he'd got just two pounds of the seven left.

"There's plenty of food here," said Francis kindly. "My God, there goes the phone again."

The phone had been ringing ever since Gray got back. People couldn't come or wanted to know if they could bring friends or couldn't remember where Francis lived.

"So you're moving in here," said Charmian, vigorously washing tomatoes.

Gray shrugged. Was he? "Only for a few weeks."

"My mother invited a friend for the weekend once and she stayed three years. You're very neurotic, aren't you? I notice you jump every time the phone rings."

Gray cut himself a piece of cheese. He was just thinking what a snorter of a letter he'd write them about those Yugoslavian rights when Francis came back into the kitchen, his expression concerned, rather embarrassed. He came up to Gray and laid a hand on his shoulder.

"It's your stepfather. Apparently, your mother's very ill. Will you go and talk to him?"

Gray went into the living room. Honoré's broken English rushed excitedly at him out of the receiver. "My son, I try to find you at your house but always the telephone is occupy, so I remember me you go to the house of Francis and I find the number—Oh, the difficulty of finding him!"

"What is it, Honoré?" said Gray in English.

"It is Mummy. She die, I think."

"You mean, she's *dead?*"

"No, no, *pas du tout.* She have a grand *paralyse* and the doctor Villon he is with her now and he say she die very soon, tomorrow, he don't know. He wish her go to the hospital in Jency but I say no, no, not while old Honoré have breath and force to take care of her. You come, *hein?* You come today?"

"All right," said Gray, a hollow feeling at the pit of his stomach. "Yes, sure I'll come."

"You have the money, you carry him with you? I give you sufficient money to go with the plane for Paris and then the bus for Bajon. So you fly with him this day from Eetreau and I see you tonight at Le Petit Trianon."

"I'll come straightaway. I'll go home and get my passport and then I'll come."

He walked back into the kitchen. The others were sitting at the table, silent, wearing long faces as suitable to the occasion.

"I say, I'm awfully sorry about your mum," said Charmian gruffly.

"Yes, well, of course," said Francis. "I mean, if there's anything we can do . . ."

There was something he could do but Gray postponed asking him for a few minutes. He knew very well that people who make this offer at times of bereavement or threatened bereavement seldom intend to do anything beyond producing sympathy and a drink.

"I'll have to miss the party. I'd better go now if I've got to get to the hovel before going to the airport."

"Let me give you a drink," said Francis.

The whisky, on a more or less empty stomach, gave Gray courage. "There is one thing you could do," he said.

Francis didn't ask him what it was. He sighed slightly. "I suppose you haven't got the money for your fare."

"All I've got between me and the dole is about two quid."

Charmian said, but not unkindly, "Oh, God."

"How much would it be?"

"Look, Francis, I'm expecting a cheque any day. It'll only be a short-term loan. I know I've got money coming because I've sold some Yugoslavian rights."

"You can't get money out of Communist countries," said Charmian briskly. "Writers never can. My mother's got a friend who's a *very famous* writer and he says publishers have to pay so much tax or something that they just leave the money in banks in places behind the Iron Curtain."

It was like a jet of cold water hitting him in the face. It didn't occur to him to doubt what she said. He remembered now hearing remarks very like hers from Peter Marshall at one of those convivial lunches, only Peter had added, "If you do sell in Yugoslavia, say, we'll leave the money in our account in Belgrade and maybe you can have a holiday there sometime and spend it." Pity Honoré didn't live in Belgrade . . .

"Christ, I'm in a hell of a mess."

Francis said again, "How much would it be?"

"About thirty-five pounds."

"Gray, you mustn't think I'm not sympathetic, but how the hell d'you think I'm going to lay my hands on thirty-five quid on a Sunday? I don't have more than five in the flat. Have you got any money, lovey?"

"About two, fifty," said Charmian. Having apparently decided that the period of empathetic grieving was over, she had resumed her eating of ham and lettuce.

"I suppose I'll have to go down to the tobacconist and see if he'll cash me a cheque."

Gray phoned the airport and was told there was a flight at eight thirty. He felt stunned. What was going to happen when he got back from France? When the cheque came he'd have about sixteen pounds but he'd owe thirty-five to Francis, and then there was going to be the business of giving Francis another nine pounds a week to share this bloody greenhouse. Oblivious of the girl, he put his head in his hands and closed his eyes . . .

Inevitably, he began to think how different his situation would have been if he'd agreed to what Drusilla had required of him a year ago. Of course he'd still be going to Bajon, that and that only would be the same. But he wouldn't have been dependant on other people's charity, despised by this girl, the object of Francis's contempt, always worried out of his wits over money . . .

A touch on his shoulder jerked him out of this reverie. "Bear up," said Francis. "I've got you the thirty-five."

"Thanks. I'm very grateful, Francis."

"I don't want to press you at a time like this but the thing is it doesn't leave me much to spare, and what with these few days in Devon and the rent and everything, if you could see your way . . . ?"

Gray nodded. It seemed pointless to make promises about quick repayment. He wouldn't be able to put conviction into his voice and Francis wouldn't believe him if he did.

"Have a good party."

"We'll drink to you," said Francis. "Absent friends."

Charmian lifted her head and managed a half-hearted farewell smile. And Francis's own expression was indulgent but impatient too. They'd both be glad to get rid of him. The red glass door closed with a relieved bang before he was halfway down the path.

If he'd done what she'd asked, he thought, he'd be in a taxi now, proceeding from his luxury flat to a first-class seat in an aircraft, his pigskin luggage up there beside the driver, his pockets full of money. He'd be like Tiny who, she'd once said, always carried huge sums about on him, ready to pay cash for what he wanted. And in Bajon the chambermaids would be preparing for him the best bedroom with private bath at the Écu d'Or. Above all, he'd have been free from worry.

It seemed to him as he waited for his train that all his troubles had come upon him because he hadn't done what she'd asked and conspired with her to kill her husband.

CHAPTER 9

Although he'd been preoccupied with thoughts of money throughout that long journey, it wasn't until he was back at the hovel that
he remembered his mother's will. Under it, he was to inherit half
her property. Well, he wouldn't dwell on that, it was too base.
Pushing away the thought with all its attractions and all its at-
tendant guilt, he packed some clothes, put his royalty statement
into the strongbox and got out his passport. There didn't seem
any point in locking the strongbox, so he just closed the lid, leaving the key in. Was there anything else he had to do before leaving for France, apart from putting the phone back on the hook?
He did this, but at the back of his mind there remained something
else. What? Not put Jeff off. He'd be back by next Saturday, and
Francis would take him in all right when he knew he was heir to
half his mother's money. No, this was some engagement, some
duty . . . Suddenly he remembered—Miss Platt's party. On his
way back down the lane he'd call on Miss Platt and tell her he
wouldn't be able to go.

Seen from the gate, the hovel looked as if it hadn't been in-
habited for years. Its weatherboard soaked by seasons of rain,
scaled and bleached by sun to the texture of an oyster shell. It lay
deep in its nest of bracken, a decaying shack behind whose windows hung faded and tattered cotton curtains. Silver birches,
beeches with trunks as grey as steel, encroached upon it as if trying to conceal its decrepitude. It had a lost abandoned look as of
a piece of rubbish thrown into the heart of the Forest along with
the rest of the trippers' litter. But it was worth fifteen thousand
pounds. Miss Platt had said so. If Mal were to put it up for sale,
he'd get rid of it that same day for this huge, this unbelievable,
sum.

He found the lucky vendor in her front garden, cutting early roses.

"Aren't we having a lovely warm spell, Mr. Lanceton? It makes me more sorry than ever I have to leave."

Gray said, "I'm afraid I shan't be able to come to your party. I've got to go to France. My mother lives there and she's dangerously ill."

"Oh, dear, I *am* sorry. Is there anything I can do?" Miss Platt put down her scissors. "Would you like me to keep an eye on The White Cottage?"

But for the letters to Tiny, Gray might have forgotten this was the hovel's real name. "No, thanks. I haven't anything worth pinching."

"Just as you like but it wouldn't be any trouble and I'm sure Mr. Tringham would take over from me. I do hope you'll find your mother better. There's no one like one's mother, is there? And worse for a man, I feel."

As he went down the lane, past the Willises' churned-up lawn, past the new estate and out into the High Beech Road, he thought about what she'd said. "There's no one like one's mother" . . . Since Honoré's phone call, he'd thought a lot about money, about Drusilla and money, about his mother's money, but he hadn't really thought about his mother herself at all. Did he care for her? Did it matter to him at all whether she lived or died? In his mind he had two mothers, two separate and distinct women, the woman who had rejected her son, her country, and her friends for an ugly little French waiter, and the woman who, since her first husband's death, had kept a home for her son, loving him, welcoming his friends. It was of this woman—lost to him, dead for fourteen years—that Gray tried to think now. She had been a friend and companion rather than a parent and he had mourned her with the bitter bewilderment of a fifteen-year-old, unable to understand—he understood now all right—the power of an obsessive passion. Understanding doesn't make for love, only for indifferent forgiveness.

He'd mourned her then. But, because she wasn't really two women but only one, he couldn't grieve now for the broken creature who was dying at last, not his but Honoré's, the property of Honoré and of France.

Flying to Paris was nothing to Tiny, no more than driving down to Loughton High Road. He flew to America, Hong Kong, Australia; to Copenhagen for lunch and back home for dinner. Once, Gray remembered now, he'd flown to Paris for the weekend . . .

"You'll be able to come and stay with me at the hovel. We can have the whole weekend together, Dru," he'd said.

"Yes, and it'll give us a chance to take the acid."

"I thought you'd forgotten all about that."

"How little you know me. I never forget anything. You can get some, can't you? You said you could. I hope you weren't just bragging to impress."

"I know a bloke who can get me some acid, yes."

"But you're going to be all moralistic and bloody upstage about it? Damn you, you make me sick! What's the harm? It's not addictive, it's anti-addictive. I know all about it."

From reading pop paperbacks, he'd thought, with sections entitled *The Weed* and *Club des Haschischins* and *A New Perception*. "Look, Dru, I just happen to believe it's wrong to use a drug like LSD just for playing, for sensation-seeking. It's quite another thing when it's used in psychotherapy and under supervision."

"Have you ever taken it?"

"Yes, once, about four years ago."

"Christ, that's marvellous! You're like one of those crappy old saints who went to orgies every night until they were about forty and then turned on everybody else and told them sex was sin just because they'd got past it themselves. *God!*"

"It wasn't a nice experience. It may be for some people but it wasn't for me."

"Why shouldn't I try it? Why you and not me? I've never done anything. You're always stopping me when I want to have experiences. I shan't come here at all if you won't get the acid. I'll go to Paris with Tiny and, my God, won't I live it up while he's at his stupid old seminar. I'll pick up the first guy that makes a pass at me." She leaned towards him then, wheedling, "Gray, we could take it together. They say it makes sex wonderful. Wouldn't you like that, me even more wonderful than I am?"

Of course he'd got the acid. There was very little he wouldn't have done for her except that one thing. But he wasn't going to take it himself. That was dangerous. One to take it, one to be there and watch, to supervise and, if necessary, to restrain. For, although the stable personality may react no more than to see distortions (or realities?) and experience a heightening of certain senses, the unstable may become violent, manic, wild. Drusilla, whatever she was, however much he might love her, was hardly stable.

It was early May, just over a year ago, the east wind sharp and chill. On the Saturday morning they had gone into his bedroom and he'd given her the acid while the wind howled around the hovel and, up above them somewhere, Tiny's plane flew away to France. Massive Tiny in his eighty-guinea suit leaned back in his first-class lushly cushioned seat, taking his double Scotch from the air hostess, opening his *Financial Times*, reading, having no idea, no idea at all, of what was taking place those thousands of feet below him. Serene, innocent Tiny, who had never for a moment suspected . . .

> "*And many a man there is, even at this present,*
> *Now while I speak this, holds his wife by th'arm,*
> *That little thinks she has been sluiced in's absence,*
> *And his pond fished by his next neighbour,*
> *By Sir Smile, his neighbour . . .*"

Gray felt a shiver run through him. It was ugly when put like that, for he had been Tiny's neighbour, in the geographical as well as the ethical sense, had even pointed out the fact in the first of those letters. He'd been Sir Smile, Tiny's neighbour, who had fished his pond in his absence—how coarse and clinical was that Jacobean imagery!—and had scarcely considered the man as a person except when it came to drawing the line at the farthest limit.

Well, it was past now, and he and Tiny, the sparer and the

spared, perhaps both betrayed in their absence by a neighbour, that smiling tennis player . . .

Gray blocked off his memories. Beneath him now he could see the lights of Paris. He fastened his seat belt, put out his cigarette and braced himself for further ordeals ahead.

The aircraft was late and the one available bus took him only as far as Jency, ten miles from Bajon, but he thumbed an illegal hitch the rest of the way. The only lights still on in Bajon were those of the Écu d'Or, haunt of Honoré, the mayor, and M. Reville, the glass manufacturer. Honoré, however, would hardly be there now. Gray looked at his watch, striking a match to do so, and saw it was close on midnight. Strange to think that at this time twenty-four hours before he'd been in Marble Arch tube station phoning Drusilla.

He went past the clump of chestnut trees, past the house called Les Marrons and down the little side road which would, after the bungalows, finally peter out as miserably as Pocket Lane itself into fields, woods, and the farm named Les Fonds. Honoré's was the fourth bungalow. A light was on in a front room. By this light Gray could see the sheet of green concrete spread over and crushing every growing thing that might have protruded its head, the plastic-lined pond, and around the pond, the brightly coloured circus of gnomes, frogs fishing, coy naked infants, lions with yellow staring eyes and fat ducks, which was Honoré's great pride. Mercifully, the light was too dim to show the alternating pink and green bricks of which the bungalow was built.

Not for the first time Gray reflected on this extraordinary anomaly in the French nation, that they who have contributed more to the world's art in music, in literature, in painting, than perhaps any other race and have been the acknowledged arbiters of taste, should also possess a bourgeoisie that exhibits the worst taste on earth. He marvelled that the French who produced Gabriel and Le Nôtre should also have produced Honoré Duval, and then he went up to the door and rang the bell.

Honoré came running to answer his ring.

"Ah, my son, at last you come!" Honoré embraced him, kissing him on both cheeks. He smelt, as usual, very powerfully of garlic.

"You have a good fly? Don't be unquiet now, *ce n'est pas fini*. She lives. She sleeps. You see her, no?"

"In a minute, Honoré. Is there anything to eat?"

"I cook for you," said Honoré enthusiastically. It was a fervour, Gray knew, which would soon wane and be replaced by wily suspiciousness. "I make the omelette."

"I only want a bit of bread and cheese."

"What, when I not see you three, four years? You think I am that bad father? Come now to the kitchen and I cook."

Gray wished he hadn't mentioned food. Honoré, though French and an ex-waiter, one who had moved for two-thirds of his life among French *haute cuisine* and in the ambience of its tradition, was an appalling cook. Aware that French cooking depends for much of its excellence on the subtle use of herbs, he overdid the rosemary and basil to an inedible degree. He also knew that cream plays an important part in most dishes but he was too mean to use cream at all. This would have been less unbearable if he had cooked egg and chips or plain stews but these he scorned. It must be the time-honoured French dishes or nothing, those traditional marvellous delicacies which the world venerates and copies—only with the cream and wine left out and packet herbs thrust in by spoonfuls.

"Extinguish, please," said Honoré as Gray followed him tiredly into the kitchen. This was Honoré's way of telling him to put the light out. Every light had to be put out when one left a room to keep the electricity bills down. Gray extinguished and sat down in one of the bright blue chairs with scarlet and blue plastic seat. It was very quiet, nearly as quiet as in the hovel.

In the middle of the kitchen table was a pink plastic geranium in a white plastic urn and there were plastic flowers all over the windowsill. The wall clock was of orange glass with chrome hands and the wall plates which ringed it showed châteaux in relief and glorious Technicolour. All the tints of a tropic bird were in that kitchen and every surface was spotless, bathed in the rosy radiance of a pink strip light.

Honoré, who had tied an apron round himself, began beating eggs and throwing in pinches of dried parsley and dried chives until the mixture turned a dull green. Cooking demanded concentration and a reverend silence and neither man spoke for a while. Gray eyed his stepfather thoughtfully.

He was a thin spare man, rather under middle height, with brown skin and hair which had been black but now was grizzled. His thin lips were permanently, even when relaxed, curled up into a sickle-shaped smile, but the small black eyes remained shrewd and cool. He looked what he was, a French peasant, but he looked more so; he looked like a French peasant in a farce written by an Englishman.

Gray had never been able to fathom what his mother had seen in him but now, after three years' separation, he began to understand. Perhaps this was because he was older or perhaps it was because he had only in those years really known the power of sex. To a woman like his mother, sheltered, refined even, this dark and certainly vital little man with his sharp eyes and his calculating smile, might have been what Drusilla had been to him, Gray, the embodiment of sex. He always reminded Gray of one of those onion sellers from whom his mother used to buy when they called at the house on Wimbledon Common. Could it be that Enid Lanceton, outwardly cool and civilised, had been so drawn to these small brown men with onion strings hanging from their bicycles, that she longed to find one for herself? Well, she'd found him, Gray thought, looking at Honoré, his plastic flowers and his curtains patterned with yellow pots and pans, and she'd paid very dearly for her find.

"*Voilà!*" said Honoré, slapping the omelette down on a green and red checked plate. "Come now, eat her quick, or she grow cold."

Gray ate her quick. The omelette looked like a cabbage leaf fried in thin batter but it tasted like a compost heap and he gobbled it down as fast as he could, hoping in this way to avoid those pauses in eating in which the full flavour might make itself felt. There was a faint sound in the bungalow which reminded him of the regular whirr, rising and falling, of a piece of machinery. He couldn't think what it was but it was the only sound apart from the clatter Honoré was making at the sink.

"Now for some good French coffee."

Good coffee was the last thing one got at Le Petit Trianon. Honoré scorned instant which all his neighbours now used but his avarice jibbed at making fresh coffee each time it was needed. So once a week he boiled up a saucepanful of water, coffee, and chicory, and this mixture, salt and bitter, was heated up and served till the last drop was gone. Gray's stomach, which digested Swedish meatballs, ravioli, and canned beef olives with impunity, revolted at Honoré's coffee.

"No, thanks. I shan't be able to sleep. I'll go in and see Mother now."

Her bedroom—their bedroom—was the only room she had managed to keep unscathed from her husband's taste. The walls were white, the furniture plain walnut, the carpet and covers sea-blue. On the wall above the bed hung a painted and gilded icon of a Virgin and Child.

The dying woman lay on her back, her hands outside the counterpane. She was snoring stertorously, and now Gray knew what was the dolorous, regular sound he had heard. It had been machinery, the machinery of Enid Duval's respiration. He approached the bed and looked down at the gaunt, blank face. He had thought of her as two women but now he saw that there were three, his mother, Honoré's wife, both absorbed in this third and last.

Honoré said, "Kiss her, my son. Embrace her."

Gray took no notice of him. He lifted one of the hands and held it. It was very cold. His mother didn't stir or change the rhythm of her breathing.

"Enid, here is Gray-arm. Here is your boy at last."

"Oh, leave it," said Gray. "What's the point?"

His English deserting him, Honoré burst into an excited Gallic tirade. Gray caught only the gist of it, that Anglo-Saxons had no proper feelings.

"I'm going to bed. Good night."

Honoré shrugged. "Good night, my son. You find your room O.K., *hein?* All day I run up and down, the work is never done, but I make time for arranging clean drapes for you."

Used to Honoré's curious and direct rendering of French terms into English, Gray knew this meant he had put clean sheets on the bed. He went into "his" room which Honoré had furnished as suitable for the son of the house. It was mainly blue—blue for a boy—magenta roses on the blue carpet, yellow daffodils on the blue curtains. The one picture, replacing a *pietà* Gray had once told his stepfather he loathed, showed Madame Roland in a blue gown standing on the steps of a red and silver guillotine and uttering, according to the caption beneath, O *Liberté, que de crimes on commis en ton nom!*

The truth of this was evident. Many crimes were committed in the name of liberty, his mother's marriage for instance. For liberty Drusilla had contemplated a crime far more horrible. Gray thought he would probably stay awake dwelling on this but the bed was so comfortable—the best thing about Le Petit Trianon, the most comfortable bed he ever slept in, vastly superior to the one at the hovel or Francis's or the one by the window at the Oranmore—that he fell asleep almost immediately.

CHAPTER 10

He was awakened at seven by a racket so furious that at first he thought his mother must have died in the night and Honoré had summoned the whole village to view her. Surely no one could make so much noise getting breakfast for three people. Then, under the cacophony, as it were, he heard the rhythm of her snoring and understood that Honoré, who never seemed tired, was using this method of indicating it was time to get up. He rolled over and, though he couldn't get back to sleep, lay there defiantly till eight when the door flew open and a vacuum cleaner charged in.

"Early to bed and early to rise," said Honoré merrily, "make him wealthy, healthy, and wise. There, I know the English proverb."

Gray noticed he'd put "wealthy" first. Typical. "I didn't get to bed early. Can I have a bath?"

At Le Petit Trianon you couldn't count on there being hot water. A bathroom there was with fishes on the tiles and a furry peach-coloured cover on the lavatory seat; a large immersion heater there was also, but Honoré kept this switched off, washing up from heated kettles. If you wanted a bath you had to book it some hours or even days in advance.

"Later," said Honoré. In very colloquial French, he went on to say something about electricity bills, the folly of too much bathing and—incredibly, Gray thought—that he had no time at present to turn on the heater.

"Sorry, I didn't get that."

"Aha!" His stepfather wagged a finger at him while energetically vacuuming the room. "I think you don't know French like you say. Now you are here you practise him. Breakfast waits. Come."

Gray got up and washed in water from a saucepan. The cheap cheese-coloured soap Honoré provided stung his hand so that he almost cried out. In another saucepan was coffee, on the table half a *baguette*. The custom of the French is to buy these bread sticks freshly each morning but Honoré never did this. He couldn't bear to throw anything away and old *baguettes* lingered till they were finished up, even though by then they looked and tasted like petrified loofahs.

After Dr. Villon had called and pronounced no change in his patient, Gray went down to the village to get fresh bread. Bajon hadn't altered much since his last visit. The Écu d'Or was still in need of painting, the brown-grey farm buildings still slumbered like heavy old animals behind brown-grey walls. The four shops in the postwar parade, wine shop, baker, butcher, and general store-post office, were still under the same management. He walked to the end of the village street to see if the bra advertisement was still there. It was, a huge poster on a hoarding showing two rounded mountains encased in lace, and the words, *Desirée,* Votre *Soutien-gorge.* He retraced his steps, went past Honoré's turning, past two new shops, past a hairdresser ambitiously called *Jeanne Moreau, Coiffeur des Dames,* and came to the road sign, *Nids de poules.* When he'd first come to Bajon he'd thought this really meant there were hens' nests in the road, not just potholes, but Honoré had corrected him, laughing with merry derision.

The day passed slowly and the slumbrous heat continued. Gray found some of the books his mother had brought with her from Wimbledon and settled down in the back garden to read *The Constant Nymph.* The back garden was a lawn ten metres by eight on which Honoré had erected three strange objects, each being a tripod of green-painted poles surmounted by a plaster face. Three chains hung from the poles bearing a kind of urn or bucket filled with marigolds. Gray couldn't get used to these elaborate and hideous devices, designed with such care and trouble to display such small clusters of flowers, but the sun was warm and this a way of passing the time.

At about eight Honoré said that a poor old man who was on his feet from morning till night, worn out as cook, nurse and general manager, deserved a little relaxation in the evenings. Gray, he was sure, would stay with Enid while he went to the Écu for a *fine.*

Several neighbours had called during the day to offer their services as sitters but Honoré had refused them, saying Gray would like to remain with his mummy.

Enid maintained her regular unbroken snoring while Gray sat beside her. He finished *The Constant Nymph* and began on *The Blue Lagoon.* Honoré came in at eleven, smelling of brandy and with a message from the mayor that he longed to meet the author of *Le Vin d'Étonnement.*

In the morning Father Normand appeared, a stout and gloomy black figure whom Honoré treated as if he were at least an archbishop. He was closeted for a long time with Gray's mother, only leaving the bedroom on the arrival of Dr. Villon. Neither priest nor doctor spoke to Gray. They had no English and Honoré had assured them that Gray had no French. The week-old chicory concoction was served and the two elderly men drank it with apparent pleasure, complimenting Honoré on his selfless devotion to his wife and pointing out to him (Father Normand) that he would find his reward in heaven, and (Dr. Villon) that he would find it on earth in the shape of Le Petit Trianon and Enid's savings. Since Gray wasn't supposed to be able to understand a word of this, they spoke freely in front of him of Enid's imminent death and Honoré's good fortune in having married, if not for money, where money was.

Gray wouldn't have put it past him to help Enid towards her end if she lingered on much longer. He showed no grief, only a faint unease at the mention of money. The priest and the doctor praised him for his stoical front, but Gray didn't think it was stoicism. Honoré's eyes flashed with something like loathing when he was feeding Enid or sponging her face, and when he thought Gray wasn't looking.

How many husbands and wives were capable of murder in certain circumstances? A good many, maybe. Gray had hardly thought of Drusilla since he'd arrived in France. There was nothing here to evoke her. He hadn't been to France since becoming her lover so he hadn't even the memory of remembering her while there. Nor had she ever been near the place. She and Tiny holidayed in St. Tropez and St. Moritz—those patron saints of tourism—or further and more exotically afield. But he thought of her now. When he considered spouses as murderers, he could hardly fail to think of Drusilla.

When had she first mentioned it? In March? In April? No, because she hadn't taken the acid till May . . .

It took about half an hour to work. Then she began to tell him what she saw, the old beamed bedroom vastly widened and elongated so that it seemed to have the dimensions of a baronial hall. The clouds outside the window became purple and vast, rolling and huge as she had never seen clouds before. She'd got up to look more closely at them, distressed because the window wasn't a hundred feet away but only two yards.

She was wearing an amethyst ring, its stone a chunk of rough crystal, and she described it to him as a range of mountains full of caves. She said she could see little people walking in and out of the caves. He wouldn't make love—it seemed wrong to him, unnatural—and she didn't seem to mind, so they went downstairs and he cooked her lunch. The food frightened her. She saw the vegetables in the soup as sea creatures writhing in a pool. After that she sat still for a long time, not telling him any more until at last she said:

"I don't like it. It's bending my mind."

"Of course. What did you expect?"

"I don't feel sexy. I've got no sex any more. Suppose it doesn't come back?"

"It will. The effects will wear off quite soon and then you'll sleep."

"What would happen if I drove the car?"

"For God's sake, you'd crash! Your sense of distance would be all messed up."

"I want to try. Just in the lane."

He had to hold her back by force. He'd known something like that might happen but he hadn't realised she was so strong. She struggled, striking him, kicking at his legs. But in the end he got the car key away from her, and when she was calmer they went out for a walk.

They walked in the forest and saw some people riding ponies. Drusilla said they were a troop of cavalry and their faces were all cruel, cruel and sad. He sat down with her under a tree but the birds frightened her. She said they were trying to get at her and peck her to pieces. Early in the evening she'd fallen asleep, waking once to tell him she'd dreamed of birds attacking Tiny's aircraft and pecking holes in it till Tiny fell out. One of the birds was herself, a harpy with feathers and a tail but with a woman's breasts and face and long flowing hair.

"I can't understand people taking that for *fun*," she said when she left for home the next night. "Why the hell did you give it to me?"

"Because you nagged me into it. I wish I hadn't."

Many times he'd wished he hadn't, for that wasn't the end of the nagging but only the beginning. That was when it had begun. But it didn't matter now, it was all the same now . . .

"Raise yourself, my son. You are having a dream?"

Honoré spoke jovially but with a hint of reproof. He expected young people—especially young people without means of support—to leap to their feet whenever their seniors entered or left a room. Dr. Villon and Father Normand were leaving, lost in admiration apparently of Honoré's linguistic ability. Gray said *au revoir* politely but remained where he was. Out in the hall he could hear Honoré waving away their compliments with the explanation that anyone who had been for years in a managerial situation in the international hotel business was bound to have several languages at his tongue's end.

After the evening meal—canned lobster bisque with canned prawns and bits of white fish in it that Honoré called *bouillabaisse*—he went for a walk down the road as far as Les Fonds. There were nearly as many gnats and flies as in Pocket Lane. In fact, the place reminded him of Pocket Lane except for the persistent baying of the farmer's chained dog. Gray knew that French country people like to keep their dogs chained. Presumably the animals get used to it, presumably this one would be let loose at night. But for some reason the sight and sound disquieted him deeply. He didn't know the reason. He couldn't think why this thin captive sheepdog, straining at its chain, barking steadily, hollowly and in vain, awakened in him a kind of chilly dread.

When he got back Honoré was spruce in dark jacket, dark cravat and beret, ready for his *fine*.

"Give my love to the mayor."

"Tomorrow he come here to call. He speak good English—not

so good as me, but good. You must stand when he come in, Gray-arm, as is respectable from a young boy to an old man of honour and reason. Now I leave you to give Mummy her coffee."

Gray hated doing this, hated supporting Enid, who smelt and who dribbled, on one arm while with the other hand he had to force between her shaking lips the obscene feeding cup with its spout. But he couldn't protest. She was his mother. Those were the lips that had said—long, long ago—"How lovely to have you home again, darling," those the hands that had held his face when she kissed him goodbye, sewn the marking tags on his school clothes, brought him tea when he awoke late in the holidays.

As he fed her the hot milk with a trace of coffee in it, watching perhaps a quarter of the quantity go down her throat while the rest slopped onto the coverlet, he thought she was weaker than she had been on the previous evening, her eyes more glazed and distant, her flesh even less pliant. She didn't know him. Probably she thought he was someone Honoré had got in from the village. And he didn't know her. She wasn't the mother he'd loved or the mother he'd hated, but just an old Frenchwoman for whom he felt nothing but repulsion and pity.

The relationship between mother and son is the most complete that can exist between human beings. Who had said that? Freud, he thought. And perhaps the most easily destroyed? She and Honoré and life itself had destroyed it and now it was too late.

He took away the cup and laid her down on the pillows. Her head lolled to one side and she began to snore again, but unevenly, breathily. He'd never seen anyone die but, whatever Honoré or the doctor might say, whatever false alarms, reassurances, anticlimaxes, there had been in the past, he knew she was dying now. Tomorrow or the next day she would die.

He sat by her bed and finished *The Blue Lagoon*, relieved when Honoré came back and she was still alive.

All the next day, Wednesday, Enid went on dying. Even Honoré knew it now. He and Dr. Villon sat in the kitchen, drinking coffee, waiting. Honoré kept saying something which Gray interpreted as meaning he wouldn't wish it prolonged, and he was reminded of Theobald Pontifex in *The Way of All Flesh* who had used those words when his own unloved wife lay on her death-bed. Gray found *The Way of All Flesh* among his mother's books and began to read it, although it was a far cry from his usual reading matter, being a great novel and such as he used to prefer.

Father Normand came in and administered Extreme Unction. He left without taking coffee. Perhaps yesterday's dose had been too much for him or else he thought it a frivolous drink and unsuitable to the occasion. The mayor didn't come. By now the whole village knew that Enid was really dying at last. They hadn't loved her. How could they love a foreigner and an English-woman? But they all loved Honoré who had been born among them and who, when rich, had returned humbly to live in the village of his birth.

That night Honoré didn't go to the Écu, though Enid slept a little more peacefully. He vacuumed the whole house again, made more green omelettes and finally switched on the heater for Gray's bath. Wrapped in a dragon-decorated dressing gown belonging to his stepfather, Gray came out of the bathroom at about eleven, hoping to escape to bed. But Honoré intercepted him in the hall.

"Now we have the chat, I think. We have no time till now for the chat, *hein?*"

"Just as you like."

"I like, Gray-arm," said Honoré, adding as Gray followed him into the living room. "Extinguish, please."

Gray turned off the hall light behind him. His stepfather lit a Disque Bleu and recorked the brandy bottle from which he had been drinking while Gray was in the bath.

"Sit down, my son. Now, Gray-arm, you know of—how do you say?—Mummy's legs?"

Gray stared at him, then understood. For one grotesque moment he'd thought Honoré was referring to Enid's lower limbs, the French for legacy having eluded him.

"Yes," he said warily.

"Half for you and half for me, yes?"

"I'd rather not talk about it. She's not dead yet."

"But, Gray-arm, I do not talk of it, I talk of you. I am unquiet only for what become of you without money."

"I shan't be without money after . . . Well, we won't discuss it."

Honoré drew deeply on his cigarette. He seemed to ponder, looking sly and not altogether at ease. Suddenly he said loudly and rapidly, "It is necessary for you only to write more books. This you can do, for you have talent. I know this, I, Honoré Duval. Just a poor old waiter, you say, but a Frenchman, however, and all the French, they *know*." He banged his concave chest. "It is in-built, come in the birth."

"Inborn," said Gray, "though I doubt that." He'd often noticed how Honoré was a poor old waiter when he wanted something and an international manager when out to impress.

"So you write more books, come rich and undependant again, *hein?*"

"Maybe," said Gray, wondering where all this was leading and determined to let it lead nowhere. "I'd rather not talk about any of this. I'm going to bed in a minute."

"O.K., O.K., we talk of this at other time. But I tell you it is bad, bad, to hope for money come from anywhere but what one works. This is the only good money for a man."

People who live in glass houses shouldn't throw stones, thought Gray. "We were going to talk of something else."

"O.K., very good. We talk of England. Only once I visit England, very cold, very rainy. But I make many friends. All Mummy's friends love me. So now you tell me, how goes Mrs. Palmer and Mrs. 'Arcoort, and Mrs. Ouarrinaire?"

Resignedly, Gray told him that while the first two ladies were no longer within the circle of his acquaintance, Mal's mother was, as far as he knew, still well and happy in Wimbledon. Honoré nodded sagely, his composure recovered. He stubbed out his cigarette and lit another.

"And how," he said, "goes the good Isabel?"

CHAPTER 11

Gray too had been lighting a cigarette. He'd taken the match from Honoré and held it downwards to steady the flame. Now he let it fall into the ashtray and took the cigarette from his lips.

"Isabel?" he said.

"You look unquiet, Gray-arm, like you see the phantom. Perhaps you have too much hot water in your bath. Take a blanket from your bed or you will be enrheumed."

Gray said automatically, the words having no meaning or sense for him, "I'm not cold."

Honoré shrugged at the folly of the young who never take advice. Speaking French, he began to extol Isabel, praising her English strength of character, her intrepidity as a spinster *d'un certain age* in going by herself to Australia.

Getting up stiffly, Gray said, "I'm going to bed."

"In the centre of our chat? I see. O.K., Gray-arm, do as please yourself. Manners make man. Another English proverb. Strange that these English proverbs make nonsense to English persons."

Gray went out and banged the door, ignoring Honoré's command to extinguish the hall light. He shut himself in his room and sat on the bed, his body really cold now and convulsed with gooseflesh.

Isabel. Christ, how had he come to forget about Isabel? And he'd only just forgotten. He'd almost remembered as he was leaving the hovel. He'd known there was something to remember and he'd thought it was Miss Platt's party. As if it mattered a damn whether he went to her party or not. All the time it was Isabel. Shades of memory had flitted across his mind, making him faintly cold and sick, as when he'd walked down to the farmyard at Les Fonds. Was it possible he'd made another mistake, got the wrong weekend?

In the kitchen there was an old copy of *Le Soir*, Friday's. He went out there and found it lining the scarlet pedal bin. *Vendredi, le quatre juin,* and there the photograph of the floods in some remote antipodean city that had certainly been last Friday's main news. If Friday was the fourth, today, the following Wednesday, was June the ninth, and Monday had been the seventh. Anyway, it was pointless checking. Isabel's day was the day he'd been due back from Francis's party.

He slumped down at the table, pressing his hands so hard against his head that the burnt palm began to throb again. What the hell was he going to do, trapped here in Bajon, without money, with his mother dying?

He tried to think coolly and reasonably about what must have happened. At midday on Monday, June the seventh, Isabel must have driven down Pocket Lane in her Mini. She'd have let herself into the hovel with the key he'd given her, opened the kitchen door, left on the bath cover a dozen or so cans of meat, placed on the floor a small pan of water and, after kisses and farewells, gentle pats and promises to return after not too long a time, left Dido, the Labrador bitch, alone and waiting.

Gray will be back soon, she'd have said. Gray will take care of you. Be a good dog and sleep till he comes. And then she'd hung the key up on the hook, shut the kitchen door and driven to Heathrow, to an aircraft, to Australia . . .

It was unthinkable, but it must have happened. What was there to have stopped it happening? Isabel knew she'd find an empty house, closed-up, neglected, shabby. That was how she'd expect to find it. He'd left nothing to indicate he'd gone to France, told no one but Miss Platt who, even if she'd been in her garden, wouldn't know Isabel, still less accost a stranger to gossip about her neighbours.

The dog, that was the important thing. Dido, the dog with the lovely face and what he'd thought of as kind eyes. God, they wouldn't be kind now, not after she'd been locked in that hole without food and only about half a pint of water for more than two days, but wild and terrified. There was food beside her, food ironically encased in metal which even the most persistent fangs and claws couldn't reach. At this moment those fangs and claws would be tearing at the bolted back door, the larder door, the cellar door, until in exhaustion she took refuge in baying, roaring with far more need and agony than the farmer's chained dog.

There was no one to hear her. No one would come down the lane till Mr. Tringham passed on Saturday evening . . . Gray got up and went back to the living room where Honoré was still sitting, the brandy bottle once more uncorked.

"Honoré, can I use the phone?"

This was a request far more momentous than merely asking for a bath. Honoré used the phone to speak to his stepson perhaps three times a year on matters of urgency and, almost as rarely, to summon Dr. Villon. It stood in his and Enid's bedroom, between their beds. Actually getting one's hands on it was more difficult than obtaining the use of the phone trolley in a crowded hospital.

Having cast upon him a look of reproachful astonishment, Honoré said in elementary slow French that the phone was in Enid's room, that to disturb Enid would be a sin, that it was ten minutes to midnight and, lastly, that he had thought Gray was asleep.

"It's urgent," said Gray, but without explanation.

Honoré wasn't going to let him get away with that. Whom did he wish to phone and why? Answering his own question, he suggested it must be a woman with whom Gray had made a date he now realised he couldn't keep. In a way this was true, but Gray didn't say so. Honoré proceeded to tell him, firstly, that calls to England were of a cost *formidable* and, secondly, that any woman one could phone at midnight couldn't be virtuous and the relationship he supposed Gray was having with her must therefore be immoral. He, Honoré Duval, wouldn't give his support to immorality, especially at midnight.

Gray thought, not for the first time, how absurd it is that the French whom the English think of as sexy and raffish should in fact be morally strict while believing the English sexy and depraved. "This," he said, trying to keep his patience, "is something I've forgotten to do in the rush of coming here, something to do with Isabel."

"Isabel," said Honore, "has gone to Australia. Now go to your bed, Gray-arm, and tomorrow we see, *hein?*"

Gray saw it was useless. Whom could he phone, anyway? In his panic, he hadn't thought of that. At this hour there wasn't anyone he could phone and he told himself, still feeling sick and cold, that there was nothing to be done till the morning.

He couldn't sleep. He tossed from side to side, sometimes getting up and going to the window until the dawn came and the chained dog began to bark. Gray flung himself face-downwards on the bed. A doze that was more dream than sleep came to him at about five, the dream he often had in which Drusilla was telling him she wanted to marry him.

"Will you ask Tiny to divorce you?" he'd said as he was saying now in the dream.

"How can I? He wouldn't, anyway."

"If you left him and stayed away for five years he'd have to whether he wanted to or not."

"*Five years?* Where'll we be in five years? Who's going to keep me? You?"

"We'd both have to work. They talk about unemployment, but there's plenty of work if you don't mind what you do."

Her white hands, beringed, that had never done heavier work than put flowers in a vase, whisk cream, wash silk . . . She stared at him, her thin pink mouth curling.

"Gray, I can't live without money. I've always had it. Even before I was married I always had everything I wanted. I can't imagine what life'd be if I couldn't just walk into a shop and buy something when I wanted it."

"Then we go on as we are."

"He might die," she said. "If he dies it'll all be mine. It's in his will, I've seen it. He's got hundreds of thousands in shares, not a million but hundreds of thousands."

"So what? It's his. What'd you do with it if it were yours, anyway?"

"Give it to you," she said simply.

"That's not my tough little Dru talking."

"Damn you! Damn you! I *would*."

"What can I do about it? Kill him for you?"

"Yes," she said.

He lurched awake, bathed in sweat, muttering, "I couldn't kill anyone, anything. I couldn't kill a fly, a wasp . . ." and then he remembered. He couldn't kill anything but he was now, at this moment, killing a dog. With that thought came simultaneously a tremendous relief, a knowledge, sudden and satisfying, that it was all right, that Isabel wouldn't have left Dido there after all. Because she'd have met the milkman. She was coming at twelve and she was always punctual; the milkman too was always punctual and came at twelve, except on Fridays when he was later. The milkman knew he was away and would have told Isabel. She'd have been very cross and put out but she wouldn't have left the dog.

He fell at once into a profound and dreamless sleep from which he was awakened at about eight by the pompous measured tones of Dr. Villon. The snoring was no longer audible. Gray got up and dressed quickly, rather ashamed to be so relieved and happy when his mother was dying and perhaps now dead.

Enid wasn't dead. A spark of life clung to that otherwise lifeless body, showing itself in the faint rise and fall of her chest under the bedclothes. He did what Honoré had urged him to do but what he wouldn't do in his stepfather's presence, kissed her gently on the sunken yellowish cheek. Then he went into the kitchen where Honoré was repeating to the doctor that he wouldn't wish it prolonged.

"*Bonjour,*" said Gray. "*Je crois qu'il fera chaud aujourd'hui.*"

The doctor took this to indicate Gray's having received a miraculous gift of tongues and burst into a long disquisition on the weather, the harvest, tourism, the state of French roads, and the imminence of drought. Gray said, "Excuse me, I'm going out to get some fresh bread."

His stepfather smiled sadly. "He does not understand, *mon vieux.* You are wasting your breath."

Bajon lay baked in hard white sunlight. The road was dusty, showing in the distance under the bra advertisement (*Desirée.* Votre *Soutien-gorge*) shivering mirages above the potholes. He bought two bread sticks and turned back, passing a milkman on a cart. This milkman wore a black T-shirt and a black beret but, in spite of his Gallic air, he had something of the look of Gray's own milkman, and this impression was enhanced when he raised one hand and called out, "*Bonjour, monsieur!*"

Gray waved back. He'd never see his own milkman again and he'd miss him more than anyone else in Pocket Lane. It had been rather nice and touching the way his milkman had shaken hands with him when they'd said goodbye and . . .

God! He'd forgotten that. Of course Isabel wouldn't have seen the milkman because he wasn't calling any more. Gray had paid him and said goodbye. And he wouldn't even be down that end of the lane. He'd said that was the one good thing about losing Gray's custom, not having to go all the way down the lane again. Oh, *God*. He'd snatched those few hours of sleep on the strength of utter illusion. Things were just as they'd been last night, only worse. Dido *was* in the hovel and now—it was half-past nine—she'd been there for nearly seventy hours.

He felt almost faint, standing there in the heat, the *baguettes* under his arm, at the enormity of it. He wanted to run away and hide somewhere, hide himself for years on the other side of the earth. But it was ridiculous thinking like that. He had to stay and he had to phone someone and *now*.

But who? Miss Platt, obviously. She lived nearest. She was a nice kindly woman who probably loved animals but wasn't one of those censorious old bags who'd relish lecturing him on his cruelty and then broadcasting it about. And she was practical, self-reliant. She wouldn't be afraid of the dog who had by now very likely lost all her gentleness in fear and hunger. Why had he been such a fool as to stop Miss Platt when she'd offered to keep an eye on the hovel? If only he'd agreed none of this would have happened. Useless thinking of that now. The only thing to think of was somehow getting hold of Miss Platt's number.

"How pale is your face!" said Honoré when he put the bread down on the kitchen table. "It's the shock," he said in French to Dr. Villon. "He mustn't be ill. What will become of me if I have two *malades* on my hands?"

"I'd like the phone, Honoré, please."

"Ah, to telephone the bad lady, I think."

"This lady is seventy years old and lives next door to me in England. I want her to see to something at my house."

"*Mais le télèphone se trouve dans la chambre de Mme. Duval!*" exclaimed Dr. Villon who had picked up one word of this.

Gray said he knew the telephone found itself in the room of his mother but the lead on it was long and could be taken out into the hall. Muttering about *formidable* expense, Honoré fetched the phone and stuck it on the hall floor. Gray was getting directory enquiries when he remembered that Miss Platt wouldn't be there. Today was Thursday and she'd moved.

He mustn't despair over a thing like that. There were other people. Francis, for instance. Francis wouldn't like it but he'd do it. Anyone but a monster would do it. No, on second thoughts, Francis couldn't because he'd gone to Devon with Charmian. Jeff, then. Jeff had the van to get him there fast. Good. After a long delay, Gray heard the distant burr-burr of the phone ringing in Tranmere Villas. Jeff was the perfect person to ask, not censorious or thick either, not the kind to want a string of explanations or to make a fuss about breaking in. Whoever went would have to do that as he, Gray, had one key, the other was on the hook, and the third . . .

When he'd heard twenty burr-burrs and got no answer, he gave up. No use wasting time. Jeff must be out with the van. Who else was there? Hundreds of people, David, Sally, Liam, Bob . . . David would be at work and God knew where he worked; Sally had gone to Mull; Liam was among the dozens of friends Jeff said had left London; Bob would be at a lecture. There was always Mrs. Warriner. He'd heard of her from Mal but not actually seen her for three years. He couldn't bring himself to phone a sixty-year-old Wimbledon lady who had no car and ask her to make a twenty-mile journey.

Back to Pocket Lane, review the scene there. Pity he hadn't chatted up the library girl or got to know some of the people on the estate. Mr. Tringham had no phone. That left the Willises. His courage almost failed him, but there was no help for it. A quickly flashing picture of Dido collapsed on the floor, her swollen tongue extended from bared teeth, and he was asking the operator to find him Mrs. Willis's number.

"Oueeleece," repeated the operator. Surely there could hardly be a more difficult name for a Frenchwoman to get her tongue round. "Will you please spell that?"

Gray spelt it. Burr-burr, burr-burr . . . She was going to be out too or on holiday. The whole world was away. He slumped on to the floor and put his hand up to his damp forehead. Click, and she answered.

"Pocket Farm."

"I have a call from Bajon-sur-Lone, France."

"Yes, all right. Who is that?"

"Mrs. Willis? This is Graham Lanceton."

"*Who?*"

"Graham Lanceton. I'm afraid we had a bit of a disagreement when last we met. I live at the White Cottage and the thing is . . ."

"Are you the person who had the nerve to let the cows into my garden? Are you the man who insulted me with some of the vilest language I ever heard in my . . . ?"

"Yes, yes, I'm extremely sorry about that. Please don't ring off."

But she did. With a shrill, "You must be mad!" she crashed down the receiver. Gray cursed and kicked the phone. He went back to Honoré and the doctor and poured himself a cup of coffee. Honoré gave him a sideways smile.

"So? You succeed?"

"No." He longed to tell someone about it, to have the views of someone else, even someone as hopelessly unsuitable as his stepfather. Honoré was narrow and bourgeois, but the bourgeois often know what to do in emergencies. Sitting down, he told Honoré what had happened and how he had failed.

Utter mystification clouded Honoré's face. For a moment he was stupefied, silent. Then he translated everything Gray had said for the benefit of the doctor. Rapidly and incomprehensibly they discussed the matter for a while, shaking their heads, shrugging and waving their hands about. Finally Honoré said in English, "Your mummy die and you are unquiet for a dog?"

"I've told you."

"For a *dog!*" Honoré threw up his hands, cackled, said to Dr. Villon in slower and readily understandable French, "I know it is a cliché to say so but the English are all mad. I who married one am forced to admit it. They are mad and they love animals more than people."

"I shall go and attend my patient," said Dr. Villon, casting upon Gray a frown of contempt.

Gray returned to the hall. All warmth had passed from his body and he was shivering. He must rescue the dog and he must phone someone to effect this rescue for him. There was only one person left.

She was the obvious person and, strangely, the best fitted for the job. She wouldn't hesitate or be afraid. She had a key. She lived near enough to be there in a quarter of an hour.

It was a Thursday. On a Thursday they had first become lovers and on a Thursday they had parted. Thursday had always been their day, Thor's day, the day of the most powerful of the gods.

He sat on the floor, not touching the phone, not yet, but confronting it, facing it as if for a duel he knew it would win. It was immobile, expectant, complacent, waiting for him to yield to it. And, though silent, it seemed to be saying, I am the magic, the saviour, the breaker of hearts, the go-between of lovers, the god that will give life to a dog and draw you back to bondage.

CHAPTER 12

A stream of sunshine poured through the frosted glass of the front door, almost blinding him. In such bright, early summer light she'd stood that morning in the hovel kitchen where Dido now was. She was so beautiful and the light so brilliant that the dazzlement of both had hurt his eyes. Wide-eyed, undisturbed by the sunlight because it was behind her, she'd said, "Yes, why not? Why not kill him?"

"You're joking. You're not serious."

"Aren't I? I've even worked out how to do it. You'll get him here and give him some acid like you gave me, only he won't know. Give it to him in tea. And then when he leaves—you'll have to time that carefully—he'll crash. He'll go over the top of the Wake roundabout."

"Apart from the fact that I wouldn't, it's absurd. It's so old-hat, freaking people out with acid for a joke."

"Damn you, it's not a joke! It'd work."

He'd laughed as one laughs with embarrassment at other people's fantasies, and said with a shrug, shifting out of the light into sane cool shadow, "You do it, then, if that's the kind of thing you fancy. He's your bloke. You give him acid and let him crash his car in Loughton High Road, only don't expect me to get it for you."

"Gray . . ." The hand in his, the thin scented lips against his neck, his ear, "Gray, let's talk about it. As a joke, if you like, but let's *see* if it could be done. We'll pretend we're the sort of unhappy wife and her lover you read about in murder books. Mrs. Thompson and Bywaters or Mrs. Bravo and her old doctor. Let's just talk, Gray."

He jerked to his feet and out of the blazing light as his mother's own old doctor came out of the sickroom. Dr. Villon threw up his hands, sighed, and went into the kitchen. Gray squatted down again, took off the phone receiver and immediately replaced it. He couldn't talk to her. How could he even have considered it? There must be other people, there must be someone . . . But he'd been through all that before and there wasn't.

The only thing to do was to put the whole thing into cold practical terms, to forget all those dreams he'd had of her and those total recall reconstructions, and tell himself plainly what had happened and what he was doing. Well, he'd had a love affair and a very satisfying one, much as most people do sometime in their lives. It had ended because the two of them weren't really compatible. But there wasn't any reason why they couldn't still be friends, was there? If he was going to go through life being afraid of meeting every woman he'd had any sort of relationship with, it was a poor look-out. It was ridiculous to get neurotic over talking to an old friend.

An old friend? *Drusilla?* No more of that . . . He could sit here all day arguing with himself and all the time the dog was in there, starving, maybe going mad. Once more he'd talk to her, just once. In some ways it might actually do him good to talk to her. Very probably hearing her voice—talking to him, not like that Marble Arch one-sided thing—and hearing the stupid ignorant things she'd say would cure him of her once and for all.

With a half-smile, blasé, a little rueful (the rake giving his discarded mistress a ring for old times' sake) he picked up the receiver and dialled her number. He dialled the code and the seven digits. It was all so simple. His hand was trembling which was rather absurd. He cleared his throat, listening to the number ringing, once, twice, three times . . .

"Yes?"

His heart turned over. He put his hand to it as if, stupidly, he could steady its turbulence through ribs and flesh. And now the temptation to do what he'd done on Saturday night, to breathe only, to listen and not to speak, was nearly overpowering. He closed his eyes and saw the sunshine as a scarlet lake, burning, split by meteors.

"Yes?"

Again he cleared his throat which felt bone dry yet choked with phlegm.

"Drusilla." That one word was all he could manage but it was enough. Enough to cause utter deep silence, broken at last by her sigh, a long rough sound like a fingernail drawing across silk.

"You took your time," she said slowly, enunciating each word with great care; then briskly, shockingly, and in her old way, "What d'you want?"

"Dru, I . . ." Where was the rake, the casual caller-up of old girl friends? Gray made a grab at this errant Don Juan who had never really been an alter ego, tried to speak with his voice, "How are you? How have you been all these months?"

"All right. I'm always all right. You didn't ring me up to ask that."

Don Juan said, "No, I rang you as an old friend."

"An old what? You've got a nerve!"

"Dru . . ." Firmly now, remembering nothing but the dog, "I'm ringing you to ask you to do me a favour."

"Why should I? You never did me any."

"Please listen, Dru. I know I've no right to ask anything of you. I wouldn't do this if it wasn't—terribly urgent. There's no one else I can ask." It was easy after all, easy after the first initial shock. "I'm in France. My mother's—well, dying." And then he told her about it, as he'd told Honoré but more succinctly.

A sort of soft vibrant moan came down the line. For a moment he thought she was crying, not at the pathos of the story, but for them, for what they'd lost. There came a gasp and he knew she was laughing.

"What a fool you are! You make a mess of everything."

"But you will go there, won't you?"

A pause. A gust of smothered laughter. He was talking to her quite ordinarily and pleasantly and she was laughing also quite ordinarily and pleasantly. It was hard to believe.

"I'll go," she said. "Haven't much choice, have I? What am I supposed to do with it when I get it out?"

"Could you get her to a vet?"

"I don't know any bloody vets. Oh, I'll find one. I think you've lost your mind."

"Quite possibly. Dru, could you—will you call me back at this number? I can't call you because my stepfather freaks out if I keep using the phone."

"I'll phone you. Tonight sometime. I'm not surprised about your stepfather. You haven't any money, that's your trouble, and when people haven't any money other people treat them like children. It's a rule of life."

"Dru . . . ?"

"Yes?"

"Nothing," he said. "You'll call me back?"

"Didn't I say I would?" The phone went down hard. He hadn't had a chance even to say goodbye. She never said it. Not once could he remember her ever saying the word goodbye. He scrambled to his feet, went into the bathroom and was sick down the loo.

Enid was snoring irregularly. Otherwise the house was silent. Gray lay on his bed in the blue room whose closed curtains couldn't shut out the blaze of noon. Mme. Roland remarked to him scornfully, aloof in the face of the scaffold, "O Liberty, what crimes are committed in thy name!"

Well, he'd done it and it hadn't been too bad. The sickness was only natural after the release of so much tension. He'd spoken to his discarded mistress and the dog would be rescued. Cool and practical, he was becoming almost what Honoré or Isabel would call a mature grown-up person. Well, well. *C'est le premier pas qui coûte:* as Honoré might say, and he'd got over the first step which counted. No harm would be done at this juncture, however, in reminding himself by another one of those reconstructions of the ugliness he'd escaped and the pitfall there still might be.

"Suppose we were serious," he'd said, "I don't see how we'd get him here."

"That's easy. You write him a letter."

"What sort of letter? 'Dear Tiny, if you'll pop over one afternoon, I'd like to give you some acid to make you crash your car. Yours truly, G. Lanceton.'"

"Don't be so bloody stupid. He collects coins, doesn't he? He's always advertising for coins in some rag called *Numismatists' News*. Get the typewriter, go on."

So he'd got the typewriter to humour her.

"Now I'll dictate. Put your address and the date, June the sixth."

She'd looked over his shoulder, her hair against his face. "Now write, 'Dear Sir, As a fellow numismatist . . .' No, that won't do. 'Dear Sir, in reply to your advertisement . . .' Sometimes he advertises in *The Times*. Oh, God, get a fresh bit of paper."

How many attempts had they made before they got the letter that satisfied her? Three? Four? At last, the final, perfect one. "Dear Sir, in reply to your advertisement in *The Times*, I think I have just what you are looking for. Since my home is not far from yours, would you care to come over and see it? Four o'clock on Saturday would be a suitable time. Yours faithfully . . .'"

"And how am I supposed to sign it?"

"Better not put your real name."

He signed it Francis Duval. She folded it up and made him type the envelope: *Harvey Janus Esq., Combe Park, Wintry Hill, Loughton, Essex.*

His indulgent smile growing rather stiff, rather sick, he'd said, "I don't have any old coins, Dru."

"I'll give you one. He's got lots of worthless coins he keeps in a box, things he thought were valuable when he first started collecting. I'll give you a Roman denier."

"Then he'd know I wasn't serious."

"Of course. So what? He'll think you just don't know. He'll say that's not what he wants and you'll say you're sorry but now he's here can you give him a cup of tea?"

"Dru, I'm getting a bit tired of this game."

O, Liberty, what crimes . . . The doorbell was ringing. Gray got off the bed because no one was answering it. There was a note on the hall table: *Depart to village for shopping. Make care of Mummy. Honoré.* He opened the door. A stout elderly man in a grey suit and grey Homburg stood there. Gray recognised the mayor whom Honoré on some previous occasion had pointed out to him across the street.

"*Entrez, monsieur, je vous en prie.*"

The mayor said in English which was very beautifully pronounced, very nearly perfect, "Mr. Graham Lanceton? I saw your stepfather in the village and he told me it would be convenient to call. How is your poor mother?"

Gray said there was no change. He showed the mayor into the living room. After what Honoré had said, the mayor's command of English struck him almost dumb. But that was typical of Honoré who, with unbounded arrogance, had probably convinced himself he was the superior linguist. Sensing his astonishment, the mayor said, with a smile; "Many years ago I spent a year in your country. I was attached to a company in Manchester. A beautiful city."

Gray had heard otherwise but he didn't say so. "I believe you—er, wanted to give me your views on my book." Might as well get it over at once.

"I should not presume, Mr. Lanceton. I am not a literary critic. I enjoyed your novel. It recalled to me happy memories of Manchester."

Since *The Wine of Astonishment* was set exclusively in Notting Hill, Gray couldn't quite understand this but he was relieved to be spared the criticism. The mayor sat silent, smiling, apparently perfectly at ease.

Gray said, "Would you care for some coffee?"

"I thank you, no. If there were perhaps some tea?"

If only there were! No packet of tea had ever found its way into Le Petit Trianon. "I'm afraid not."

"It is of no importance. It was not for coffee or tea or the discussion of contemporary literature that I came."

Why had he come, then? The mayor sat in easeful silence for quite a minute. Then he leant forward and said slowly, "Your stepfather is a gentleman of great vitality. Ebullience is, I think, the word."

"Well, it's *a* word."

"A man of impulse and one who, I think I may say, is inclined somewhat to our national vice, common among our peasantry of —shall I name it?—avarice. What matters one small vice among so many virtues?"

The mayor's English grew more expert and semantically involved with every sentence. It recalled to Gray the speech of solicitors in Victorian novels. He listened, puzzled but fascinated.

"A desire too to acquire something for nothing or almost nothing, a need to cast bread upon the waters and harvest whole loaves."

"I'm afraid I don't follow you, monsieur."

"Ah, perhaps not. I will abandon metaphor, I will make a long story short. You expect, I understand, when something happens to your mother—this English euphemism I find so tactful, so gentle—to be her heir?"

Taken aback, Gray said, "I shall inherit half, yes."

"But half of what, Mr. Lanceton? Listen, if you will be so good. Let me explain. Half of what your poor mother leaves when she passes on—you see, I know you English do not care for the strict cold expression—half will be, to put it bluntly, half of this bungalow!"

Gray stared. "I don't understand. My mother had a good deal of money invested when she remarried and . . ."

"'Had,'" interrupted the mayor urbanely, "is the operative word. Let me be quite open and aboveboard with you. M. Duval reinvested this money, speculated, if you will. There was a mine, I believe, a railway to be built that, alas, was not built. You may imagine."

Gray imagined. He knew nothing about the stock market except what everyone knows, that it is easier to lose there than to gain. But he didn't feel at all sick or angry or even very disappointed. How had he believed there would ever be any real money from any source for him?

"So you see, Mr. Lanceton," said the Victorian solicitor, "that were you to claim your inheritance, as you would be within your rights to do, you would only deprive an ageing man of the very roof over his head. This, I am sure, you would not do."

"No," said Gray rather sadly, "no, I wouldn't do that."

"Good. Excellent." The mayor got up, still smiling. "I was sure my words would be effectual. We speak," he added with a slight pedantic laugh, "the same language."

"How will he live?" asked Gray, shaking hands.

"He had the forethought, poor gentleman, to purchase a small annuity."

He would. "Goodbye," said Gray.

"I will not be so optimistic as to wish your mother recovered health, Mr. Lanceton, but say only that we must hope her suffering will not be prolonged."

They must have arranged to meet somewhere and chew over the results of the interview, for when Honoré returned with his full shopping bag, he was truly, to use the mayor's word, in an ebullient mood. He actually embraced Gray.

"My son, my boy! How goes the bad lady? You make contact with her? And the poor animal?"

Gray said, with a sense of unreality, that everything was all right now.

"Then I make the lunch. *Croque Monsieur* for us today."

"No, I'll do it." Even this simple, though grandly named, dish wasn't safe in the hands of Honoré who would be sure to add herbs and garlic to the cheese. "You go and sit with Mother."

Poor Honoré. Poor, indeed. Slicing up cheese, Gray reflected on the strange calm he felt, the lightness of heart even. Honoré while rich had been hateful to him, a kind of King to his Hamlet. For Honoré poor he had a fellow feeling. The bath water watching, the shouts of Extinguish, please! the phone fanaticism—weren't they, after all, only the sort of economies he too was forced to practise? It amused him to think of those two, Honoré and the mayor, screwing up their courage to tell him the truth, afraid of his righteous anger. But it hadn't angered him at all. Probably he'd have done the same in Honoré's place, blued all his money on a bubble and then sent some braver deputy to confess it to his judge.

No, he wasn't angry. But he was a bit ashamed of himself for mentally accusing Honoré of wanting to make away with his wife. Not every marriage partner was a Drusilla.

"Drusilla," he'd said, "I've had enough of this. It's as stupid as mooning over what you'd do if you won the pools."

"No, it isn't. You can't fix the pools. You can fix this. Just let me post that letter. I've still got it."

"It's out of date."

"Write another, then. What's the date? July the first. 'Dear Sir, In reply to your advertisement . . .'"

"I'm going out. I'm going for a walk. It's no fun being with you if all you can do is play this stupid game."

"It's not a game, it's serious."

"All right," he'd said. "So it's serious. Once and for all, will you listen to me? Leaving morality out of it, it wouldn't work. Probably he wouldn't die. He'd feel strange, see distortions and park the car. He'd ask the first motorist he saw to go to the police and the first person they'd come to'd be me."

"You don't know him. He always drives very fast. He wouldn't be able to stop in time. And they wouldn't know about you because I'd get hold of the letter and burn it."

"Burn it now," he'd said.

He shook himself and looked at Honoré who sat at the opposite side of the table, eating toasted cheese. His eyes were bright and darting but not, Gray suddenly realised, the malicious eyes of a potential killer. Honoré lacked the intelligence to be wicked. And Gray realised too that all the time he'd been at Le Petit Trianon he hadn't done a thing to help until today when he'd made the lunch. Honoré had done it all and, on the whole, done it well.

"Why don't you go out for a bit?" he said. "You need a change. Take your car."

The Citroën was hardly ever used. It lived in the garage under a nylon cover, coming out once a week to be polished. But Gray understood that now too.

"Where will I go?"

"See a friend. Go to the cinema. I don't know."

Honoré threw up his hands, smiled his monkey smile. "I don't know too, Gray-arm."

So they sat together in Enid's room, waiting for her to die. Gray read *The Way of All Flesh* intermittently. He held his mother's hand, feeling very calm, very tranquil. His mother was dying but he no longer had any reason to hope for her death. He had no money to keep him from working, to lull him into idle security. The dog would be safe now. Drusilla would phone him soon, he'd thank her and they'd say their last dignified goodbyes. Even she would say goodbye. It was wonderful to feel so free, to know that no crimes need be committed to secure liberty.

The evening was close as if a storm threatened—not tonight perhaps or tomorrow but soon. Honoré had gone to the Écu, assured by Gray that this would be good for him, that no useful purpose could be served by his staying with Enid.

Gray, who had been at peace since noon, as if his physical sickness had provided a more than physical catharsis, began to feel a gradual mounting of tension. He had meant to sit outside among the gnomes or the tripods. Provided he left the doors open, he'd hear the phone when it rang, for he'd placed it on the hall floor near the kitchen door. But, although he went into the garden, he couldn't concentrate on the last chapters of his book.

It was Thursday and Tiny went to his Masons on Thursdays at about six. She could have phoned him then. Why hadn't she? He told himself that it was only the dog's fate that was worrying him. He was concerned only for the dog and for Isabel. Drusilla was what he'd called her that morning, a discarded mistress, interesting only as an old friend might be when doing him a favour.

It was Thursday. Very likely she still turned her Thursday evenings to good account, possibly with what's-his-name, the tennis guy, Ian Something. Perhaps she was with him now and wouldn't phone till he'd gone. Gray pondered this idea, found it particularly unpleasant and went back into the house. The farmer's dog had stopped barking. No doubt it had been let off its lead. It was almost too dark to make out the shape of the phone which, doglike, was also attached to a lead, a wire stretched through the crack in the door.

Ten o'clock. He looked in on his mother who had ceased to snore, who lay on her back with her mouth open. Suppose Drusilla didn't phone? Suppose, in order to be revenged on him, she'd promised to see about the dog and then deliberately done nothing? He could phone her. If he was going to he'd better be quick, for another half hour and it would be too late for safety. But she'd phone him. She never changed her mind and she always did what she undertook.

He stood over the phone, directing his will on it, telling it to ring, ring. He clenched his fists, tensed his muscles, said to it, "Ring, damn you. Ring, you bastard!"

It obeyed him immediately and rang.

CHAPTER 13

When he had coped with the stream of idiomatic French which issued from the receiver, when he had told M. Reville, the glass manufacturer, that his mother remained the same and that Honoré had gone to the Écu, he uncorked the brandy bottle and drank some. Honoré was getting everything else, after all. He oughtn't to grudge him a drop of brandy.

If she didn't phone he wouldn't be able to sleep. That was ridiculous, though, because if she hadn't been to the hovel Dido would be dead by now and all further worry pointless. He had some more brandy and put the bottle away. He wished he knew exactly what he was worrying about. Honoré was out and he could easily phone her. There was a good half hour before danger time and Tiny got home. He'd phoned her before, twice if you counted the Marble Arch time, and it was the first step that counted.

Surely he wasn't still afraid of getting involved with her again? Or maybe afraid of *not* getting involved with her? Remember what she is, he told himself, remember what she wanted you to do . . .

" 'Dear Sir, In reply to your advertisement . . . !' Put the date. It's November the twenty-first. Oh, come on, Gray. Get up then and I'll do it. Any fool can type, I suppose. My God, it's freezing in here. When he's dead and we're together all the time we'll never be cold again. We'll have a flat in Kensington and if the central heating doesn't go up to eighty we'll have it all taken out and new in."

"We aren't going to be together all the time and you know it. We're going to go on like this till one of us gets tired of the other."

"What's that supposed to mean? I didn't see any signs of tiredness upstairs just now."

He'd turned away, warming his hands at the oil heater, looking wearily at the window scummed with frost, the skeletal trees beyond, rooted in pools of water thinly crusted with ice. Round her shoulders she'd slung the red fox, coarser and brighter than her hair.

"There's more to life than sex," he said.

"Like what? Like living in a frozen slum? Like brooding about the books you don't write and the money you can't make? I'm going to do this letter and by the spring—March, say—we can be living together with all his money in a joint account. God, but my fingers are too cold to type. You do it."

"Dru, you said just now you didn't see any signs of tiredness. All right, I'm not tired of sex. I don't think I'd ever get tired of sex with you. But I'm sick and tired to my soul of you ballsing on about killing your husband. It's grotesque."

She'd crashed her hands down on the keys so that they tangled and stuck together. Her eyes were white fire.

"D'you mean me? D'you mean I'm grotesque?"

"I didn't say that but—yes, you're grotesque and stupid and a bit mad when you talk of making that poor bloke crash his car."

"Damn you! Damn you!" He'd had to hold her off, seize her hands and force them behind her to stop her long nails tearing at his face. She'd crumpled and softened, the fur falling from her shoulders, leaving her vulnerable in the thin clinging dress that was so unsuitable for the hovel. And then, of course, the inevitable. Because this was Drusilla who, naked, warm, and sinuous under the piled blankets, was anything but grotesque, anything but stupid . . .

The tape that was playing in his brain switched off sharply. Stop, stop, remember the bad times. Forget that the bad times always ended in good times until that last time. Twenty past ten. She wasn't going to phone. That bloody thing, straining on the end of its wire leash, wasn't going to ring again tonight.

He was halfway back to the cupboard where the brandy was when the bell brayed at him. He jumped, and the jump was so galvanic that it actually pained him. Then he was on the phone at a leap, crouched over it, gasping out, "Yes, Dru, yes?"

"Hi," she said.

The coolness of her voice chilled memories, blew away longing and dreading. "What happened?" he said. "Did you find her?"

"I found her." There was a long pause. "God, Gray," she said with an almost refined distaste, quite unlike her, "God, how *could* you?"

"Is she dead?" He sat on the floor, resting his head against the wall.

"No. She was alive—just."

He exhaled on a long sigh. "What happened?" he said again.

"I took some milk and chicken with me. I was a bit scared to open the kitchen door but I needn't have been, she was too weak to move. God, the stink and the muck in there! She'd got up on the sink and plastered the window with her muck and saliva—the lot."

"Oh, Dru . . ." His head had begun to bang. It was the brandy partly, and partly the shock, though he ought to have been relieved. This was the best that could have happened.

She said harshly, "Someone ought to lock you up in a cell for three days without food or water and see how you'd like it. Why didn't you phone the police, anyway?"

Why hadn't he? It was the obvious thing. "I never thought of it."

"You haven't phoned them today?"

"No, of course not."

"You just left it to me? Typical. D'you want to hear the rest? I carried her out to the car and, Christ, was she heavy. In the car I gave her some milk but she couldn't take the chicken. Then I got her to this vet."

"Which vet?"

"A guy in Leytonstone."

"*Leytonstone?* Why on earth . . . ?"

"Because I was going up to town."

"I see," he said. She always left her car in the car park at Leytonstone tube station when she was going to London. But to have gone today? It seemed heartless, too casual. And why had she gone? To buy clothes? To—meet someone? "You went to London?"

"Why not? It's not my dog, as I hastened to tell the vet. I didn't want him thinking I'd do a thing like that. You'd better have his address and see him as soon as you get back. It's twenty-one George Street. Got that?"

"Yes. Thanks. I'm very very grateful, Dru. I ought to have phoned the police, of course. I ought . . ." He broke off, fumbling in his mind for suitable words to end the conversation. She'd done the favour he'd asked of her and now was the time for those dignified goodbyes. Thanks, no hard feelings, maybe we'll meet again someday, and meanwhile thanks . . . "Well, Dru, maybe after all this trauma we'll be able to meet one of these days and—well, you know what I mean. I'll never forget what you—I mean I'll never . . ."

"After I got back from town," she said as if he hadn't spoken, "I went in and cleaned up a bit for you."

"You did what?" He remembered once having told her that the only brush she ever lifted was the one she used for mascara. And now she, those white hands of hers, had cleaned up his filthy kitchen. He could hardly believe it. "Why did you do that?"

"Why did I get the dog? Why do I do anything for you? Don't you know yet?"

Goodbye, Drusilla. Good night, sweet lady, good night. Say it, say it, Don Juan hissed at him. A tremor rose in his throat, choking him, taking away the power of speech. He rested his cheek against the wall to cool his blood-heated face.

"You don't know, do you?" Her voice was very soft now. "You don't think about my feelings. I'm O.K. when you want someone to get you out of a mess, that's all. As far as you're concerned, the rest is over and done with."

"And you know why," he whispered, "it had to be over and done with." Clinging to a shred of sanity, he said, "We had to split up. I couldn't take it."

"That? I've given all that up. It would never have worked. I see that now." She paused and said in a very low childlike voice, almost as if reluctantly, "I tried to phone you a lot of times."

His heart was pounding. "On Thursday nights?"

"Of course."

"I left the receiver off."

"Oh, you fool," she sighed. "You hopeless fool. I wanted to tell you back in January I'd given all that up. God, I was so lonely. I wanted to talk to you so much. The line was always engaged, always engaged. I thought . . . Never mind."

"Why didn't you come to me?"

"And find you with another girl?"

"There's been no other girl, there's been no one. I was alone too."

"Then we've been a pair of hopeless fools, haven't we? Frightened of each other when all the time we really . . . Oh, what's the use? You're in France and I'm here and Tiny'll be in in a minute. We'd better stop this before we say too much."

His voice returned to him powerfully and he almost shouted at her. "Too much? How could we say too much? Don't you see we've been apart all this time over a stupid misunderstanding? We've tortured ourselves over nothing . . ."

"I've got to ring off. I can hear Tiny's car."

"Don't ring off, please. Please. No, you must. Of course you must. Listen, I'll phone you in the morning. I'll phone you at nine as soon as he's gone. God, Dru, I'm so happy . . ."

A sighing whisper cut him short. "Tomorrow, then," and the phone slid delicately into silence. In the dark warm hall he sat on the floor, cradling the receiver in his hands, hearing still an echo or a memory of her voice. His heart quietened, his body relaxed like a taut spring set free to uncoil, and as happiness, pure joy, swamped him he wanted to dance and shout, run outside and sing, embrace the tripods, yell to the whole of sleeping Bajon that his love had come back to him.

Instead of doing that, he got to his feet and went into his mother's room. Enid lay on her back, breathing shallowly, her eyes closed. Once, when he'd had nothing much to tell, he'd been able to tell her everything, and she'd listened and understood. If she were aware now, conscious, would she understand? Wouldn't her own experience of passion give her empathy?

He bent over her. He said, "Mother, I'm so happy. Everything has come right for me."

Her lids moved. The wrinkled black-stained hoods lifted and half-showed her eyes. In his euphoric state, he fancied he saw recognition there, comprehension even, and in that moment he loved her again, forgiving her entirely. He took her face in his hands and pressed his lips against the corner of her mouth, kissing her as he hadn't kissed her since he was a little boy.

Mme. Roland gave him a cynical glare and he turned her picture to the wall. He didn't want her shouting her predecapitation liberty nonsense at him any more. He knew all about liberty, he'd had enough of it in the past six months. He'd taken his liberty to avoid committing a crime and now he thought he'd committed a crime against himself and Drusilla. Let Mme. Roland make what she liked of that with her histrionic *salon* philosophy.

He got into bed naked because of the heat. How long was he going to have to stay here? Days? Weeks? If only he'd got money he could fly home and see her and then come back again. That wasn't possible—but to wait here on and on while she was in England longing for him as he was longing for her? It was a pity, he thought, that uncomplicated joy lasts so short a time, that it must always give way rapidly to practicalities and plans. In the morning when he phoned her they'd have to start making plans. In the morning, too, he'd phone Jeff and tell him not to come on Saturday. Maybe he wouldn't be moving now, after all.

In a couple of weeks time, perhaps less, she'd be visiting him at the hovel again just like she used to before Christmas. And they'd discuss the dead months with laughter at their own folly, reducing Christmas as they looked back on it to a row not much bigger than any of their rows, a momentary frown on the face of love.

In the hot stuffy bedroom where no wind lifted the curtains at the open window, where the air was warm and dry at midnight, it was hard to imagine snow. But snow had come before Christmas, and on the night before the Eve, Drusilla, the red fox lady, had pelted him with snowballs, screaming, laughing, as they walked in the frozen forest. He caught her in his arms and, mouth to mouth, the snow crystals melting on warm lips, they'd fallen to make love in the drifts under the sealskin branches of the beech trees.

That was a good memory, one to hold on to now, one he wouldn't have dared recall till now when she was back with him. But the quarrel that came after? How many times had he played that tape over and over, following as it did their final act of love?

The last time, he'd thought, the last time. Now it wasn't going to be the last time. It would even cease to be associated with the quarrel, and the quarrel itself would fade down one of the alleys which debouch from the avenue of time.

He turned over, spread-eagled under the crumpled sheet. A Thursday, of course. Exactly twenty-four weeks ago tonight. No Christmas decorations at the hovel, for Christmas was to be spent in London with Francis. But the present she'd given him on the bath cover in the kitchen, the present of a silver chain on which hung a silver Hand of Fortune (since sold) and all around it the red and gold wrappings he'd torn off in his love and gratitude. He'd drawn out a ridiculous amount, far more than he could afford, to buy her *Amorce dangereuse* and she'd laughed with delight, spraying it on her red fur, although she could have bought gallons of the stuff herself and not noticed.

Into the hovel to take her perfume before driving back to Combe Park. He'd worn the chain to go out in the forest and it had fallen icy against his chest, but now, under his shirt and Arran, it was warm with his body warmth. Tiny, of course, had paid for it. Her father didn't send her a cheque more than once a year.

"So what?" she'd said, and that had been the beginning. No, for it had begun long before, but just the beginning of the final quarrel, of the end. "I'm entitled to some of what he makes, I suppose? You could look on it as wages. Don't I keep house for him and cook and sleep with him? He only pays me two thousand a year and I'm cheap at the price."

"Two thousand?" One year he'd managed to make almost that himself, but never before and never after.

"Ah, come on, Gray. Five pounds for a silver neck thing? It's only an advance, anyway. It'll all be yours soon."

"Don't start that again, Dru. Please don't."

Don't start that, he warned himself, reaching out for the glass of water he'd put by the bed. Why remember that quarrel now? She'd given it all up, she'd said so. He'd never hear her say those things again.

"Look, Gray, you sit down and listen to me. You never thought that was a game I was playing. You were as serious as me, only you haven't got as much guts as I have."

"Please don't come the Lady Macbeth bit, Drusilla."

"Well, he did it in the end, didn't he? And so will you. We'll do another letter and you can buy the acid while you're up in town."

" 'Up in town.' You sound like the chairman of the Women's Institute off for her annual shopping spree."

She was more sensitive to this kind of insult than any other, but she took no notice. "I'll give you the money."

"Thanks. The poor bastard's going to pay for his own poison, is he? I like that. It reminds one of the Borgias. A judge'll make a lot of that—'The unfortunate Harvey Janus, murdered by his wife and her lover with a hallucinogen purchased out of his own money.' Charming."

In her red fur, waterdrops gleaming on its spikes, she sat down at the typewriter to compose another letter. The oil heater on, blue flame, incandescent; snow falling thickly, silently, against the dirty windowpane.

"Dru, will you give up this idea now? Will you promise me never to mention it again?"

"No. I'm doing it for you. You'll thank me afterwards. You'll be grateful to me all the rest of your life."

The watch she'd given him showing ten past ten; the Hand of Fortune she'd given him warm against his breastbone; melted snow lying on the floor in pools.

"It's no good, Gray. I'll never give this up."

"Will you give me up?"

She was folding the letter, sliding it into an envelope. "What's that supposed to mean?"

"That I can't go on like this. It doesn't matter what we're doing, what we're talking about. With you all roads lead to killing Tiny."

"You can put a stop to that by killing him."

"No, there's another way." He didn't look at her. "I can put a stop to it by not seeing you."

"Are you trying to say you're tired of me?"

"No, I can't imagine any man being tired of you. I'm tired of *this*. I've had it, Drusilla. As it is, I'll never be able to look back on what we had, you and me, without this poisoning it all."

"You're just a spineless coward!"

"That's true. I'm too much of a coward to kill anyone and too much of a coward to stay being your lover. You're too much for me. I hate it ending like this but I knew it would. I've known it for weeks. I shan't see you again, Dru."

"Christ, you bastard! I hate you. That's what I think of your filthy Christmas present!" The flagon broke against the heater, glass flying, scented steam rising. "I was going to make you rich. I was going to give you everything you wanted."

He felt sick. The perfume made him feel sick.

"Goodbye, Drusilla. It was nice—once. It was the best I ever had."

"You bloody liar! You ungrateful, bloody liar!"

Goodbye, Drusilla, good night, sweet lady, good night, good night . . .

"Good night, Drusilla," he said aloud. "Good night, my love. I'll talk to you in the morning."

He fell at once into a dream. He was with Tiny in the fast red car. There wasn't much room for him because Tiny was so huge, filling up his own seat and half the passenger seat, and he was driving fast, zigzagging the car from side to side of the forest road. Gray tried to make him slow down but no voice came when he tried to speak. He couldn't speak and when he put his fingers to his tongue, he found it—Oh, horrible!—divided and forked like a snake's tongue, dumb, speechless, unhuman. Then the green hillock of the roundabout was upon them, green but capped with snow, and Tiny was going over it. The red car and Tiny were going over the mountain and he, Gray, was going with them. He too was trapped in the hurtling burning car, the fire engulfing him as he struggled to get out. And now someone was hammering on the roof of the car, not a rescuer but she. Drusilla was pounding on the roof of the red Bentley to make sure that both of them were dead . . .

He gasped, "Don't, don't . . . I've had enough. I want you to give me up," and then, as the dream and the flames and the snow faded, as French smell and light and stuffiness burst back, "What . . . ? Who is it? What is it?"

Broad daylight in the bedroom and someone knocking on the door. He wrapped himself in the twisted sheet. He staggered to the door and opened it. Honoré stood outside in the dragon dressing gown, his face yellow and drawn.

"What . . . ?"

"*C'est fini.*"

"I don't . . . I was asleep."

"*C'est fini. Elle est morte.*"

"She can't be dead," he said stupidly. "It can't be finished, it's only just beginning . . ." And then he knew that Honoré meant his mother, that Enid Duval had died at last.

CHAPTER 14

In a thin high voice, Honoré said, "You come and see her?"

"All right. If you like."

The yellowness had gone from Enid's skin and death had erased most of the lines. Already she looked waxen, her open eyes glazed blue china.

"You ought to close her eyes," Gray began, and then he looked at Honoré who stood at the opposite side of the bed, dulled, silent, tears falling weakly down his cheeks. "Honoré, are you all right?"

Honoré said nothing. He fell across the bed and took the dead woman in his arms. He lay there and clung to her, making soft animal moans.

"Honoré . . ."

Gray lifted him up gently and helped him into the living room. His stepfather huddled into an armchair, shaking, his head turned against the lapel of his dressing gown. Gray gave him brandy but Honoré choked on it, sobbing. "What shall I do?" he said in French. "What will become of me?"

And then Gray saw that he'd been wrong, that his stepfather had loved her. The love hadn't been all on his mother's side but had been reciprocated to the full. Not a cynical purchase but true love. And that hatred, that disgust, he'd seen in Honoré's eyes while feeding her? Wasn't that what any man would feel? Disgust not for her but for life, for the world in which such things happened, in which the woman he loved became a helpless dribbling animal. He had loved her. He wasn't a caricature, a sick joke, but a man with a man's feelings. Gray forgot that he'd resented Honoré, hated him. He felt a great surge of guilt for misunderstanding, for laughing and despising. He forgot too, just for a moment, that he wasn't Honoré's son and—although he'd never before held a man so—he took Honoré in his arms and pressed him close against himself and forgot everything but Honoré's grief.

"My son, my son, what shall I do without her? I knew she was dying, I knew she must die, but death . . ."

"I know. I understand."

"I loved her so. I never loved any woman like her."

"I know you loved her, Honoré."

Gray made coffee and phoned the doctor and then, when it was nine and the Marseille shop where she worked would be open, he phoned Honoré's sister. Mme. Derain agreed to come. Trilling r's, swallowed vowels assaulted Gray along a crackly line, but he gathered that she'd come by Monday when she'd made arrangements with her employer.

The day was going to be close and oppressive but cooler, the sun veiled by cloud. The doctor came, then Father Normand, then an old woman, a very French little old woman looking like something out of Zola, whose job was to lay Enid Duval out. Gray, who had always been treated in this house as if he were a recalcitrant fifteen-year-old, fixed in Honoré's estimation at the age he'd been when Honoré had first met him, now found himself forced to take charge. It was he who received the mayor and M. and Mme. Reville, he who interviewed undertakers, prepared meals, answered the phone. Broken, weeping intermittently, Honoré lay on the sofa, calling to him sometimes, begging him not to leave him. His English, of which he had been so proud and which he had used as a means of defying his stepson and demonstrating his authority, deserted him. He spoke only French. And now, using his native tongue exclusively, he ceased to be a farce Frenchman. He was the dignified bereaved who commanded respect. To Gray his stepfather appeared quite different and he realised he had never known him.

"You will stay with me, my son? Now she is gone you are all I have."

"You'll have your sister, Honoré."

"Oh, my sister! Forty years have passed since we lived in the same house. What is my sister to me? I want you to stay, Grayarm. Why not? Stay here where you have a home."

"I'll stay till after the funeral," Gray promised.

He was surprised at the intensity of his own grief. Even last night, when he'd loved his mother again and fully forgiven her, he'd thought that her death, when it came, wouldn't touch him. But he was weighed down, as he busied himself with the hundred and one things that needed doing, by a quite irrational feeling. He realised that during all those years there had existed at the back of his mind a hope that one day he'd be able to have it all out with her. He'd put his case and she hers, they'd explain to each other, and in those explanations their pain would be resolved. Now she was dead and he mourned her because that day could never come. He could never tell her now how she'd hurt him and she could never tell him why.

Drusilla seemed very far away. He hadn't forgotten to phone her but only deferred it. Later in the day, when all these people had gone, when the phone had stopped ringing and he'd finished the letters to England that Honoré had asked him to write, then . . .

"Mrs. 'Arcoort and Mrs. Ouarrinaire, and our dear Isabel."

"Isabel's in Australia, Honoré. I'll be back in England before she is."

"Change your mind. Stay here with me."

"I can't, but I'll stay while you need me."

He took his letters to the post. It had begun to rain. The great *camions* travelling along the road to Jency splashed muddy water against his legs. The funeral had been fixed for Monday, so he could go home on Tuesday and maybe see Drusilla that same night. It was getting a bit late to phone her now, nearly half-past five, and the weekend was coming. Maybe it would be better to delay phoning her till Monday morning—she'd understand when she knew about his mother. But would she? Wasn't the real reason for his not phoning her a fear that he couldn't take the sharp comment he was likely to get? The "So she's popped off at last" or "Has she left you anything?" He couldn't quite take that now, not even though it came from his Dru that he loved, his Dru who had changed and was going to be his forever.

He heard the phone bell before he was inside the house. Another local sympathiser probably. Honoré wasn't in any fit state to answer it. He went quickly into the room where the phone was, not looking at the empty bed whose blue cover was drawn taut and straight over a bare mattress. The window was open to blow in rain and blow out the smell of death. He picked up the receiver.

"Hi."

"Dru?" he said, as if it could be anyone else. "Dru, is that you?"

"You didn't phone," she said in a voice that seemed to contain a world of desolation.

"No." He knew his tone sounded clipped but he couldn't help it. He was bracing himself for the unkind retort. "No, I couldn't," he said. "Dru, my mother died this morning."

Not an unkind retort but silence. Then, as if she had received a shock, almost as if the dead woman had been someone she had known and loved, she said, "Oh, *no!*"

He was moved, warmed, by the consternation in her voice. All day, strangely when they were on the point of renewing their love affair, she had been more removed from him, less present, than at any time since Christmas. She'd been—he confessed it to himself now—almost a burden, an extra problem to cope with. But that appalled "Oh, *no!*" which seemed to contain more feeling and more sympathy than any long speech of condolence, touched his heart and brought a tremor to his voice.

"I'm afraid so, Dru. My stepfather's taken it very hard and I . . ."

She wailed, "You won't be able to come home now!" She sounded sick, despairing. "I can tell by your voice, you're going to stay for the funeral!"

It was wonderful, of course, to be wanted, to know she needed him so much. But he'd have felt happier if her sympathy had been pure and simple, without strings. Yet for her to be sympathetic at all . . .

"I must, Dru darling," he said. "Try to understand. Honoré needs me till his sister comes. I've promised to stay till Tuesday."

"But *I* need you," she cried, the imperious child whose wishes must always be paramount.

"God, and don't I need you? But we've waited six months. We can wait four more days. You must see this changes things."

Please God, let her not be difficult about it, not now. Let her not make a scene *now*. His happiness at rediscovering her couldn't take storms just yet. He felt he needed to carry that happiness undisturbed, unalloyed, through the next few days like a talisman;

to have it there as a quiet place to retreat to when the sadness of bereavement grew sharp and the practical tasks exasperating. He listened to her ominous silence that seemed charged with protest, petulance, resentment.

"Dru, don't ask me to break my promise."

He dreaded the phone going down, the angry crash as she hung up on him. But there was no crash, no stormy outburst, and when she broke the silence her voice had grown hard with the chill of Thursday morning.

"I'm afraid," she said, "I'll have to. I haven't told you why I phoned yet."

"Did we ever need a reason?"

"No, but this time there happens to be one. This vet wants to see you."

"Vet?" he said obtusely.

"Yes, *vet*. Remember?"

Dido. He hadn't forgotten Dido but somehow he'd thought that now she'd been rescued from the hovel and fed and given attention, everything would be all right.

"Why does he want to see me?"

"I phoned him today to check up. He says the dog's got something wrong with her liver, something bad, and she's in a very bad way. He has to talk to the owner or someone taking the place of the owner before he operates on her. Gray, you can't just leave all this to me. Don't you see, you have to take the responsibility?"

Gray sat down heavily on Honoré's bed. He was remembering Dido as he'd last seen her, so vigorous, so vital, rippling with health. There was something sickeningly ugly in the idea that he'd destroyed all that by his lack of responsibility.

"How can she have something wrong with her liver?" he said. "I mean, malnutrition, I could understand that. But something wrong with her liver? What can I do about it? How can I help by coming home?"

"He wants to see you tomorrow," she persisted. "Gray, I said you'd come. I didn't see why not. It isn't very far just to come to London. Tiny often flies to Paris and back in a day."

"Dru, don't you see how fantastic it is? You can tell him to go ahead and operate, do anything to save the dog's life. I'll pay. I'll manage to borrow the money somehow and I'll pay."

"You'll do that but you won't come home and see to it yourself? Not even if I promise to meet you at the hovel afterwards?"

His hand closed hard on the receiver and a long thrill that was almost pain passed through his body. But it was impossible . . . "I don't have the money to go in for this jet set flying about. All I have is about three quid."

"I'll pay your fare. No, don't say you won't take Tiny's money. It won't be his. I've sold my amethyst ring. And Tiny didn't give it to me, my father did."

"Dru, I don't know what . . ."

"I told the vet you'd be there at about three. Go and ask your stepfather if it'll be all right to leave him for a day. I'll hold on."

Dry-mouthed, he laid the receiver on the pillow and went into the living room. "Honoré, I've got to go home tomorrow. I'll go in the morning and be back by night."

A bitter but very non-farcical argument ensued. Why did he have to go? Where was the money to come from? What would Honoré do on his own? Finally, why didn't Gray get a job, settle down (preferably in France) marry and forget about mad, bad Englishwomen who loved animals more than people?

"I promise I'll be back by midnight and I'll stay till after the funeral. Your friends will be with you. I'll ask Mme. Reville to come to you for the whole day."

Gray left him, feeling sick because Honoré was crying again. He picked up the phone.

"All right, Dru, I'll come."

"I knew you would! Oh God, I can't believe it. I'm going to see you tomorrow. I'm going to see you!"

"I've got to see this vet first and that won't be pleasant. You'd better tell me the set-up."

"You've got the address. Just go there and talk to him at three."

"And when and where do I see you?"

"If it were only a weekday," she said, "I could come to the airport. That's not possible on a Saturday. Tiny's going to look at some house he wants to buy for his mother in the afternoon. I'll get out of that and I'll see you at the hovel at five. O.K.?"

"Can't you—can't you meet me at the vet's?"

"I'll try, but don't count on it. I should be able to drive you back to Heathrow."

"But we will have . . ." He couldn't frame what he wanted to say in the right words, the words that would make her understand. "We will have a little time together?"

She'd understood. She gave an excited chuckle. "You know me," she said.

"Ah, Dru, I love you! I'd go a thousand miles to be with you. Say you love me and that everything that's happened doesn't matter any more."

He held his breath, listening to her silence. A long long silence. He could hear her breathing shallowly as he'd breathed that night he rang her from Marble Arch. Suddenly, coolly and steadily, she spoke:

"I love you. I've decided, if you still want me, I'll leave Tiny and come and live with you."

"My darling . . ."

"We'll talk about it tomorrow," she said.

Bang, the phone went down and he was left holding the emptiness, savouring the fulness, hardly daring to believe she'd said what she'd said. But she had, she had. And he was going to see her tomorrow.

At the end of the long lane she'd be waiting for him. He'd run the length of it. He'd let himself in by the front door and the scent of her would meet him, *Amorce dangereuse*. And she'd come out to him, her arms outstretched, her hair like a bell of gold, her white hand bare of the ring she'd sold to fetch him back to her . . .

Honoré had stopped crying but he looked very sad.

"I have been thinking, you must take the car. *Si, si, j'insiste*. It is the quickest way to fetch you back soon."

"Thank you, Honoré, it's kind of you."

"But you must remember that in France we drive on the *correct* side of the road and . . ."

"I'll take great care of your car."

"*Seigneur!* It is not of the car that I am thinking but of you, my son, you who are all I have left."

Gray smiled, touched his shoulder. Yes, he must stop seeing the worst in everyone, attributing to people self-seeking motives. He must try to understand the power of love. Drusilla would have killed for love, was leaving Tiny for love just as he was abandoning Honoré for love. Oh Love, what crimes are committed in thy name . . .

"Let us have a little glass of *cognac*," said Honoré.

CHAPTER 15

The plane got to Heathrow at one fifteen. Gray bought a London A–Z Guide, leaving himself with just enough money for his tube fare to Leytonstone and his train fare to Waltham Abbey. By ten to three he was at Leytonstone station, one of those pallid, desertlike, and arid halts that abound on the outer reaches of the tube lines, and had walked round the curving tunnel into the street.

Drusilla had said nothing about a chance of meeting him there and he didn't expect her, but he couldn't help eyeing the cars parked by the kerb in the faint hope that the E-type might be among them. Of course it wasn't there. He thought of how often her feet must tread this very spot where he now was, how often she must come to this tunnel entrance on her way to London, and then he began to walk down the long street of biggish late Victorian houses, his A–Z in his hand.

Taking the back doubles that filled the area between the road where the station was and the last farflung finger of Epping Forest, he found George Street, a curving, respectable-looking terrace, which lay under the shadow of an enormous Gothic hospital. Number twenty-one bore no brass plate or anything else to indicate that a vet occupied it, but he went up the steps and rang the bell. Expecting that at any minute the door would open and an aggressive middle-aged man in a white coat, his pockets bristling with syringes and steel combs, would fall upon him with threats of the R.S.P.C.A. and certain prosecution, Gray mentally rehearsed his defence. But when the door did open—after he'd rung twice more—no mingled smells of dog and disinfectant rolled out, no veterinary veteran was waiting to excoriate him with his tongue. Instead, a smell of baking cakes and a girl holding a baby.

"I've an appointment with the vet at three o'clock."

"What vet?" said the girl.

"Isn't there a vet has his . . ." What did they call it? ". . . his surgery here?"

"You want the place up the road. It's on this side. I don't know the number. You'll see the name up."

Surely Drusilla had said twenty-one? But maybe she hadn't. He hadn't, after all, written it down. Perhaps she'd said forty-nine which was, in fact, the number of the house on which the vet's nameplate was. He was quite used to forgetting things and he no longer really wondered at his forgetfulness. His lapses were all due, he thought, to psychological blocks, defences put up by his unconscious, and these would soon go away now. The really important things he never forgot. Nothing could have made him forget his date with Drusilla at five.

The doggy smell was here all right, a thick animal reek. Finding the door on the latch, he'd walked in without ringing and was standing in the waiting room, contemplating the copies of *The Field* and *Our Dogs* and wondering what the correct procedure was, when a woman in a khaki smock came in to ask what he wanted.

"Mr. Greenberg doesn't have a surgery on Saturday afternoons," she said curtly. "We're only open for clipping and stripping."

Distant squeaks and grunts, coming from the upper regions, testified that these operations were at present being performed.

"My name is Lanceton," he said, pausing to allow for the expression of hatred and disgust which would cross her face when she realised she was in the presence of an animal torturer. "My dog—well, a dog I was looking after—you've got it here." Her face didn't change. She simply stared. "A yellow Labrador called Dido. She was brought to Mr.—er, Greenberg last Thursday."

"Brought here? We don't board dogs."

"No, but she was ill. She was left here. She was going to have an operation."

"I will check," said Khaki Smock.

She came back after quite a long time, more than five minutes. "We've no records of what you say happened. What time on Thursday?"

"Around lunchtime."

Khaki Smock said triumphantly, "Mr. Greenberg wasn't here after twelve on Thursday."

"Could you phone him or something?"

"Well, I could. It's very inconvenient. It won't be any use. He wasn't here."

"Please," said Gray firmly.

He sat down and leafed through *The Field*. Twenty-five past three. He'd have to get out of here in five minutes if he was going to make it to the hovel by five. He could hear her phoning in another room. Was it possible he'd got the name of the street wrong as well as the number? She came back at last, looking exasperated.

"Mr. Greenberg knows nothing about it."

He had to accept that. He went back into the street, utterly at a loss. The E-Type wasn't there. Drusilla hadn't managed to come and meet him. Or was she, at this moment, waiting somewhere else for him, parked outside another vet's in another street? There must be dozens of vets in Leytonstone. Well, not dozens but several. As he walked down the street the way he'd come he had the sensation of being in a dream, one of those nightmares in which one is already late for an urgent meeting or rendezvous, but everything goes wrong. Transport is irregular or delayed, people antagonistic, addresses mistaken and simply-reached goals hideously elusive.

The obvious thing was to try and get Drusilla on the phone. Tiny would be out house-hunting and maybe she'd be there and alone. He dialled her number but no one answered, so he looked through the yellow page directory for veterinary surgeons. Immediately he saw the mistake he'd made, a mistake possible only when two suburban and contiguous townships have closely similar names. Greenberg was a vet at 49 George Street, Leytonstone; Cherwell a vet at 21 George Street, Leyton. Dido was in Leyton, not Leyton*stone*.

Twenty to four. Well, he'd come over for the sake of the dog, hadn't he? That was the real purpose of his trip, and it was no good giving up just because time was getting on. Yet even now, if he gave up now, he wouldn't get to the hovel before five fifteen. He was aware of that pressure, engendering panic, which affects us when we know we shall be late for an all-important, longed-for appointment. The air seems to swim, the ground drag at our feet, people and inanimate things conspire to detain us.

He opened his A–Z. George Street, Leyton, looked miles away, almost in Hackney Marshes. He didn't know how to get there but he knew it would take at least half an hour. That wasn't to be thought of, out of the question when Drusilla would already be dressing for him, scenting herself, watching the clock. Instead, he dialled Cherwell's number. Nothing happened, no one replied. Vets, obviously, didn't work this late on Saturdays.

But the dog . . . Surely this Cherwell guy would act on his own initiative? Surely, if an operation were necessary, he'd operate with or without consent? All he, Gray, could do was phone him from France first thing on Monday morning. And now put all this vet business behind him, waste no more time on it, but get to Liverpool Street fast.

There must be, he thought, a quicker way of making this transforest journey of seven or eight miles than by going all the way back into London and out again via sprawling northern suburbs. There must be buses, if only he knew their routes and their stops. If he'd had money he could have phoned for a mini-cab. As it was, he had just enough for his train fare.

The tube seemed to go exceptionally slow and he had to wait fifteen minutes for a train to Waltham Cross. By the time it came and he was in the carriage his watch, which he had kept checking with station clocks to make sure it wasn't fast, showed twenty-five minutes to five.

Only once had she ever been late for a date with him and that had been that first time in New Quebec Street. She wouldn't be late now. By now she'd have been waiting half an hour for him, growing bewildered perhaps, distressed, as she paced the rooms, running to the window, opening the front door to look up the lane. Then, when he hadn't come and still he hadn't come, she'd say, I won't look, I'll go away and count a hundred and by then he'll have come. Or she'd go upstairs where she couldn't see the lane and scrutinise herself again in the mirror, once more comb her flying fiery hair, touch more scent to her throat, run her hands lightly, in sensuous anticipation, over the body she'd prepared for him. Count another hundred, go slowly down the stairs, walk to the window, lift the curtain, close her eyes. When I open my eyes I shall see him coming . . .

At half-past five he was at the Waltham Abbey end of the lane. There had been an accident on the corner and the police signs were still up, the police cars still there. In the middle of the road black skid marks met and converged on a heap of sand, flung down perhaps to cover blood and horror. He didn't stop to look or enquire but quickened his pace, telling himself that a man of his age ought to be able to run two miles in twenty minutes.

He ran on the hard flat surface of the metalled road, avoiding the soggy grass verges. Pocket Lane had never seemed so long, and the twists and turns in it, the long straight stretches, with which he was so familiar, seemed multiplied as if the lane were made of elastic which some hostile giant had stretched out to frustrate him. The blood pounded in his head and his throat was parched by the time he came to the point where the tarmac petered out into clay.

Under the trees where the E-Type should have been was a big dark green Mercedes. So she'd changed her car. Tiny had bought her a new one. Gray was exhausted with running but the sight of her car brought him a new impetus and he raced on, his trousers covered with yellow mud. The rain that had fallen on the other side of the Channel had fallen here too, and in the deep ruts the clay was almost liquid. This last stretch of the lane—how short it had always seemed on those nights when he had walked her back to her car! Had it really been as long as this, hundreds of yards long surely? But he could see the hovel now, the pallid hulk of it, white as the overcast sky. The gate was open, swinging slightly in the faint breeze that set all those millions of leaves trembling. He stopped for a moment at the gate to get his breath. The sweat stood on his face and he was gasping, but he'd made it, he'd done it in just under twenty minutes.

He unlocked the front door, calling before he was inside, "Dru, Dru, I'm sorry I'm so late. I ran all the way from the station." The door swung to and clicked shut. "Dru, are you upstairs?"

There was no sound, no answer, but he thought he could smell her scent, *Amorce dangereuse*. For a second he was sure he smelt it, and then it was gone, lost in the hovel smells of dust and slowly rotting wood. Breathing more evenly now, he dumped his case and shed his jacket on to the floor. The "lounge" was empty and so was the kitchen. Of course she'd be upstairs, in bed even, waiting for him. That would be like her, to tease him, to wait for him silently, giggling under the bedclothes, and then, when he came into the bedroom, break into a gale of laughter.

He ran up the staircase two at a time. The bedroom door was shut. He knew he'd left it open—he always did—and his heart began to drum. Outside the door he hesitated, not from shyness or fear or doubt, but to let himself feel fully the excitement and the joy he'd been suppressing all day. Now, when he'd reached his goal at last, he could yield to these emotions. He could stand here for ten seconds, his eyes closed, rejoicing that they were together again; stand on the threshold of their reunion, savour it and what it would mean to the full, then open the door.

Opening his eyes, he pushed the door softly, not speaking.

The bed was empty, the dirty sheets flung back as he'd left them, a cup half full of cold tea dregs on the bedside table as he'd left it, as he'd left it . . . The breeze fluttered the strips of rag that served as curtains and swayed a dust-hung cobweb. A hollowness where that full-pounding heart had been, he surveyed the empty room, unable to believe.

The spare room was empty too. He went downstairs and out into the garden where the bracken now grew as high as a man and where little weeds already greened the ash patch of his fire. No sun shone out of the white sky. There was no sound but the muted twitter of songless birds. A gust of wind ruffled the bracken tops and rustled away into the Forest.

But she must be here, her car was here. Perhaps she'd got tired of waiting and gone for a walk. He called her name once more and then he walked back down the lane, splashing through the yellow mud.

The car was still there, still empty. He went up to it and looked through its windows. On the back seat was a copy of the *Financial Times* and, lying on top of it, a spectacles case. Drusilla wouldn't have those things in her car. She wouldn't have a black leather head-rest for her passenger or a pair of very masculine-looking string-backed driving gloves on the dashboard shelf.

It wasn't her car. She hadn't come.

"You won't come? Not even if I promise to meet you at the hovel afterwards?"

That's what she'd said.

"Oh, God, I can't believe it. I'm going to see you tomorrow. I'm going to see you!"

He resisted a temptation to kick the car, the innocent inanimate thing that had nothing to do with her but probably belonged to some bird-watcher or archaeologist. Dragging his feet, his head bent, he didn't see Mr. Tringham until the old man was almost upon him and they had nearly collided.

"Look where you're going, young man!"

Gray would have gone on without making any answer but Mr. Tringham, who was for once not carrying a book and who had apparently come out of his cottage especially to talk to him, said rather accusingly, "You've been in France."

"Yes."

"There was a man in your garden earlier on. Little short chap, walking round the place, looking up at the windows. Thought you ought to know. He could have been trying to break in."

What did he care who broke in? What did it matter to him who'd been there if she hadn't? "I couldn't care less," he said.

"Hmm. I went out for my walk early, thinking it might rain later. There was this rough-looking long-haired chap sitting under a tree and this other one in your garden. I'd have called the police only I haven't got a telephone."

"I know," Gray said bitterly.

"Hmm. You young people take these things very lightly, I must say. Personally, I think we should use your phone—or Mr. Warriner's, I should say—and get on to the police now."

Gray said with irritable savagery, "I don't want the police messing about the place. I want to be left alone."

He walked away sullenly. Mr. Tringham grunted something after him about decadence and modern youth, after the manner of Honoré. Gray slammed the hovel door shut and went into the lounge, aiming a kick at the golf clubs which fell over with a clang.

She hadn't come. He'd travelled all this way to see her, travelled hundreds of miles, run the last bit till he'd felt his lungs were bursting, and she hadn't come.

CHAPTER 16

The phone clicked, then began to ring. He lifted the receiver dully, knowing it would be she, not wanting her voice or any part of her, but the whole of her.

"Hi."

"What happened?" he said wearily.

"What happened to *you*?"

"Dru, I got here at five to six. I ran like hell. Couldn't you have waited for me? Where are you?"

"I'm at home," she said. "I just got in. Tiny said he'd be home at six and I couldn't think of an excuse for not being home too. I left it till the last moment and then I had to go. He's out in the garden now but we'd better be quick."

"Christ, Dru, you promised me. You promised you'd be here. You were going to drive me to the airport. That doesn't matter but if you could have made the time for that, surely you could have . . . I wanted you so much."

"Can't be helped. I did what I could. I should have known you're always late and you always make a mess of things. You didn't even find the vet, did you?"

"How can you know that?"

"Because I rang Mr. Cherwell myself to check if you'd been."

"So it *was* Cherwell . . . ?"

"Of course it was. Twenty-one George Street, Leyton. I told you, didn't I? It's no use, anyway. The dog's had to be destroyed."

"Oh, Dru, *no!*"

"Oh, Gray, *yes*. You couldn't have done anything if you had seen Cherwell, so it's no good worrying about it. What are you going to do now?"

"Lie down and die too, I should think. I've come all this way for nothing and I haven't got a bean. If ever anyone made a pointless journey, this is it. I haven't had anything to eat all day and I haven't got my fare back. And you ask me what I'm going to do."

"You haven't found the money, then?"

"Money? What money? I've only been here ten minutes. I'm plastered with mud and dead tired."

"My poor Gray. Never mind, I'll tell you what you're going to do. You're going to change your clothes, take the money I left you—it's in the kitchen—and get the hell out of that hole back to France. Just write the day off, don't think about it. Quick now, I can see Tiny coming back up the garden."

"*Tiny?* What the hell do we care about Tiny now? If you're joining me next week, if you're coming to live with me, what does it matter what Tiny thinks? The sooner he knows the better." He cleared his throat. "Dru, you haven't changed your mind? You are going to come to me next week?"

She sighed, a fluttery trembly sound. Her words were firm but not her voice. "I never change my mind."

"God, I feel sick when I think I've come all this way and I'm not going to see you after all. When will I see you?"

"Soon. As soon as you get back. Tuesday. I'm going to ring off now."

"No, don't. Please don't." If the receiver went down now, if she ended as she always did without a farewell . . . But she always ended like that. "Dru, please!"

For the first time she said it. "Goodbye, Gray. Goodbye."

On the bath counter he found the electricity bill, the phone bill, the cheque from his publishers—the first two cancelling out the third—a postcard from Mal and, strangely enough, one from Francis and Charmian in Lynmouth. Beside all this correspondence she'd left the money for him in an untidy heap. It seemed a small heap until he looked again, saw that the notes were all tenners and that there were ten of them. He'd expected thirty pounds and found a hundred.

There was no loving note with them. She'd left a hundred pounds in a careless heap as someone else might have left twenty pence in small change; she'd sold her amethyst ring to get him money and he felt a warm, heartbeating gratitude, but he'd have liked a letter. Just a word to tell of her love for him, her distress at not seeing him. He'd never received a letter from her in all their time together and he didn't know what her handwriting looked like.

Still, he wouldn't need handwriting, mementoes, recorded evidence of her, after next week. It was getting on for half-past six and he ought to be on his way. Change these filthy clothes first, though. He went upstairs, wondering what he could find to put on, for he'd left everything dirty just as he'd taken it off.

He hadn't looked round the bedroom at all beyond looking at the bed itself. Now he saw that his dirty jeans and shirt had been washed and actually ironed and were draped over the back of the bedroom chair with his clean Arran. She'd done that for him. She'd cleaned up his kitchen and washed his clothes. Changing quickly, he wondered if she'd done that to show him she could do it, that she wouldn't be helpless, the bewildered rich girl uprooted from luxury, when she came to him. He rolled up his clay-spattered trousers and thrust them under the bath cover. The window had been polished, the paintwork washed in places. She'd done all that for him and sold her precious ring too. He ought to be on top of the world with happiness, but disappointment at not seeing her still weighed him down. Nothing she could do for him or give him made up for the lack of her.

But once back in France, he'd phone her and ask her to be waiting for him when he got home on Tuesday night. She still had her key. The one he could see hanging over the sink must be Isabel's, left there when she'd brought Dido. Guilt for the dog's death welled up inside him. His own absentmindedness had brought that about and led him to make a mistake that almost amounted to criminality. But once Drusilla was with him all that would be changed. He'd have to plan, remember, make decisions.

Just time for a pot of milkless tea and something out of a tin before he set off back to the station. The phone was on the hook, his correspondence examined, the back door bolted. Now was there anything he ought to remember? Perhaps he'd better take that spare key with him. If the little man Mr. Tringham had seen had really been a burglar, the key was in a very vulnerable position. Break one pane of glass in the window, insert a hand and reach for the hook, and the hovel, Mal's hovel, would be anyone's to do as he liked with. Mal wouldn't be too happy to have his golf clubs pinched or any of that tatty old furniture which was, after all, all he had.

Congratulating himself on this unprecedented prudence, Gray unhooked the key and was slipping it into his pocket when he paused, surprised to see how bright and shiny it was. Surely he'd given Isabel the spare key Mal had left him? This key looked more like the one he'd had specially cut for Drusilla when she'd been visiting him so often that there was a chance she'd have to let herself in before he got back from the shops. But perhaps he hadn't given her the new one. Perhaps, in fact, she'd had the old one and the shiny key had been kept for spare. He couldn't remember at all and it didn't seem to matter.

He drank his tea and left the dirty crockery on the draining board. The hundred pounds in his pocket, the two keys, he closed the front door behind him. A thin drizzle, not much more than a mist, was falling and heavier drops plopped rhythmically from waterlogged beech leaves. He walked on the wet grass to avoid the paintbox mud.

The green car was still there. Probably it was a stolen car, abandoned in this out-of-the-way spot. Or its owner had gone on some nature ramble in the forest depths. Both the Willises were in their front garden, standing on their lawn which now looked as good as new to Gray, arguing about something or commiserating perhaps with each other over a case of mildew or leaf blight. They saw Gray and turned away very stiffly, ramrod-backed.

At the corner the police cars had gone and the sand been removed. He walked quickly on towards the station.

Over France the moon was shining. Had the sky cleared in England too and was this same moon shining down on Epping Forest and Combe Park? She and Tiny would be in bed, the gross man in his black and red pyjamas reading some company chairman's memoirs or maybe the *Financial Times*, the slender girl in white frills, reading a novel. But this Saturday night there wouldn't be a phone call from a strange man, saying nothing, breathing heavily. And she wouldn't be lonely any more but thinking about how she'd have to tell the husband in the next bed she'd be leaving him next week. Dream of me, Drusilla . . .

He drove past the last *nids de poules* sign and entered sleeping Bajon, skirting the clump of chestnut trees and the house called Les Marrons. The moon gave him enough light to see by as he covered the car once more in its protective nylon. But the hall of Le Petit Trianon was pitch dark. He felt for the light switch and stumbled over something that was standing just inside the door, a bouquet of funereal lilies in a plastic urn. Afraid that the noise might have awakened his stepfather, he pushed open the bedroom door which Honoré had left ajar.

The thin moonlight, which had transformed the gnome circus into a ghostly ballet, edged the furniture with silver and made little pale geometric patterns on the carpet. Honoré, his greyish-black hair spiky and tousled, lay curled in his own bed but facing the one where Enid had slept, one arm bridging the space between, his hand tucked under her pillow. He was deeply asleep, serene, almost smiling. Gray supposed that they had always slept like that, Honoré's hand holding Enid's, and he saw that his stepfather, reality and its awfulness alienated by dreams, made belief that she lay there still and still held his hand under her cheek.

Touched, awed by the sight, Gray thought how he and Drusilla would sleep like that but in the same bed, always together. And he dreamed of her, the most tender untroubled dreams he'd ever had of her, throughout the night until the baying of the farmer's dog awoke him at eight. Then he got up and took coffee to Honoré who was neither smiling nor serene in the mornings now and whose methodical early-to-rise habits seemed to have died with Enid's death.

Mme. Reville called and carried Honoré off to Mass. Gray had the house to himself and he was alone with the phone. What did she and Tiny do on Sundays? Searching in his mind for some recollection, some account she might have given him of their usual Sunday activities, he found only a blank. Certainly they wouldn't go to church. Did Tiny perhaps play golf or drink with some equally affluent cronies in the pub that crowned the summit of Little Cornwall? There was just a chance she might be alone, or a chance even that she'd told Tiny by now and would be glad of a call from him to back her up and give her confidence.

Without further hesitation, he dialled the number. It rang and rang but no one answered. He was trying again an hour later when Mme. Reville's car drew up outside and he had to abandon the attempt. Well, he'd said Monday and surely he could wait till Monday.

The day passed slowly. Every hour now that he was away from her seemed endless. He kept thinking of the scene which might at this moment, at any moment, be taking place at Combe Park with Drusilla declaring her intention to leave and Tiny his intention of stopping her at all costs. He might even use violence. Or he might throw her out. Still, she had her key and she could take refuge at the hovel if necessary.

Honoré lay on the sofa, reading the letters Enid had written to him during the short period between their meeting and their marriage. Weeping freely, he read bits of them aloud to Gray.

"Ah, how she loved me! But so many doubts she had, my little Enid. What of my boy, she writes here, my friends? How shall I learn to live in your world, I who speak only the French I learned in school?" Honoré sat bolt upright, pointing a finger at Gray. "I crushed all her doubts with my great love. I am master now, I said. You do as I say and I say I love you, so nothing else can matter. Ah, how she adapted herself! She was already old," he said with Gallic frankness, "but soon she speaks French like a French-woman born, makes new friends, leaves all behind to be with me. With true love, Gray-arm, it can be so."

"I'm sure it can," said Gray, thinking of Drusilla.

"Let us have a little cognac, my son." Honoré bundled up his letters and rubbed at his eyes with his sleeve. "Tomorrow I shall be better. After the funeral I shall—what is it you English say? —pull me together."

After the funeral, while the company drank wine and ate cake in the living room, Gray slipped away to phone Drusilla. She'd be waiting impatiently for his call, he thought, had possibly tried to phone him earlier while they were at the church. Very likely she'd be sitting by the phone, feeling lonely and frightened because she'd had a terrible row with Tiny and now might think, because she hadn't heard from him, that her lover had deserted her too. He dialled the code and the number and heard it start to ring.

After about six double peals the receiver was lifted.

"Combe Park."

The coarse voice with its cockney inflexion, the voice that obviously wasn't Drusilla's, almost floored him. Then he realised it must be the daily woman. He and Drusilla had always had an arrangement that if he phoned and the woman answered he was to put the phone down without speaking. But not any longer surely? That didn't apply any longer, did it?

"Combe Park," she said again. "Who's that?"

Better try again later. Better not do anything now to interfere with what might be a delicate situation. He put the receiver back very carefully and quietly as if by so doing he could make belief he hadn't called Combe Park at all, and then he went back into the room where they were all talking in hushed voices, sipping Dubonnet and nibbling at *Chamonix oranges*. Immediately the mayor took him to one side and questioned him closely as to his visit to England. Had he been able to watch a Test Match or, better still, managed a trip to Manchester? Gray answered no to both, very conscious of the glare Mme. Derain had fixed on him. Her eyes were beady like her brother's and her skin as brown, but in her case the small Duval bones were concealed under a mountain of hard fat and her features buried in dark wrinkled cushions.

"*Ici,*" she said like a notice in a shop window, "*on parle français, n'est ce pas?*"

She had taken over the management of the household. It was evident that she intended to stay, to give up her job and her flat over the Marseille fish shop, for the comparative luxury and peace of Le Petit Trianon. Even more parsimonious than Honoré, she was already making plans to take in a lodger, already talking of removing the marigolds and the tripods and growing vegetables in the back garden. And English stepsons who contributed nothing to the household expenses weren't welcome to her.

One glass of Dubonnet per head was all she allowed and then the mourners were hustled away. Gray tried to phone Drusilla again and again the daily woman answered. His third attempt, made at five thirty, the last safe moment, didn't stand a chance, for Mme. Derain actually wrested the phone from his hand. She didn't moan at him or talk of *formidable* expense but said stonily that she planned to have the apparatus disconnected as soon as possible.

He'd have to try again in the morning while she was out buying bread, he thought, but when the morning came, when Honoré was drinking coffee in the kitchen, he entered the bedroom to find her already there. Ostensibly removing signs from it which would be painful to her brother, she was in fact, Gray thought, sorting out which of Enid's clothes she could convert to her own use. Gray guessed he was the type of man who would have liked to keep his dead wife's room as a shrine, each little possession of hers treasured as a reminder of their happiness. But this wasn't Mme. Derain's way. She had allowed her brother to keep Enid's wedding ring—although suggesting it would be more prudent to sell it—and Honoré held the ring loosely in his horny brown hands. It was too small to go on any of his fingers.

"I want to give you back the money you sent me," Gray said. "Here it is, thirty pounds. I want you to have it."

Honoré expostulated, but feebly and not for long. Gray foresaw his stepfather's future life as a way of crafty deception in which money would have to be slyly wrested from his sister and windfalls concealed. This was the first of them. Honoré slipped the money into his pocket but not before he had glanced, already surreptitiously, already fearfully, towards the door.

"Stay another week, Gray-arm."

"I can't. I've got a lot of things to do. For one thing, I'm going to move."

"Ah, you will move and forget to give old Honoré your new address and he will lose you."

"I won't forget."

"You'll come back for your holidays?"

"There won't be room for me when you've got your lodger."

Gray wondered suddenly if he should tell Honoré about Drusilla, give him an expurgated version perhaps, tell him there was a girl he hoped to marry when she'd got her divorce. And that was true. One day they'd be married. He wanted it that way now, open, aboveboard for all the world to see, no more secrets. He glanced at Honoré who was eating and drinking mechanically, whose thoughts were obviously with his dead wife. No, let it remain a secret for now. But it struck him as strange that he'd even contemplated telling his stepfather, his old enemy. All those years when they might have had a happy relationship they had gone out of their way each to antagonise the other, each obstinately insisting on speaking the other's language. And now, when the relationship was ending, when it was probable—and both knew it —they would never meet again, Honoré spoke French and he English and they understood each other and something that was almost love had grown up between them.

Still, one day he might come back. He and Drusilla could have their honeymoon in France, drive through Bajon—hitch through more likely, he thought—and call and see Honoré . . .

Should he try to phone her from the village? Call at the Écu and use the phone in the bar? That way they'd be able to fix a definite time for their meeting and he could have a meal ready for her and wine when she came at last to her new home and her new life.

But it would be hard to explain this action to Honoré who seemed to have an *idée fixe* that his stepson had formed a liaison with an elderly dog breeder. Why go to all that trouble, anyway, when in three or four hours he'd be in London?

"You will miss your plane," said Mme. Derain, coming in with one of Enid's scarves over her arm, a scarf that Honoré winced at the sight of. "Come now, the bus leaves in ten minutes."

"I will drive you to Jency, my son."

"No, Honoré, you're not up to it. I'll be O.K. You stay here and rest."

"*J'insiste.* Am I not your papa? Now, you do as I say."

So the nylon cover was removed from the Citroën and Honoré drove him to Jency. There they waited, drinking coffee at a little pavement café and, when the bus came, Honoré embraced him tenderly, kissing his cheeks.

"Write to me, Gray-arm."

"Of course I will."

And Gray waved from the bus until the little figure in the dark beret, the French onion seller, the waiter, the thief of his happy adolescence, the killer of his dream, had dwindled to a black dot in the wide dusty square.

CHAPTER 17

London lay under a heavy, almost unbreathable, humidity. Like
November, Gray thought, but warm. The sky was uniformly pas-
tel grey and it seemed to have fallen to lie on roofs and tree tops
like a sagging muslin bag. There was no wind, no breath of it to
move a leaf or flutter a flag or lift a tress from a woman's head.
The atmosphere was that of a greenhouse without its flowers.

He dialled her number from the air terminal and got no reply.
Probably she was out shopping. She couldn't be expected to stay
in all day just on the chance that he'd phone. At Liverpool Street
he tried again and again at Waltham Cross but each time the bell
rang into a void. Once, maybe twice, she could have been out
shopping or in the garden—but every time? He hadn't said he'd
call her but surely she'd guess he would. There was no point,
though, in getting into a state about it, rushing into every phone
box he saw on every stage of his journey. Better wait now till he
got home.

Pocket Lane had attracted to its moist dim shelter what seemed
like all the buzzing insects in Essex. Slumbrously they rose from
leaf and briar, wheeled and sang. He brushed them off his face
and off the carrier bag of food he'd bought at a delicatessen in
Gloucester Road, cold meat and salad for their supper, and a bottle of wine. Maybe she was out because she'd done what he'd wist-
fully envisaged, taken refuge from Tiny at the hovel. He hadn't
thought of ringing the hovel. She might be there waiting for him.
But no, he wasn't going to let himself in for that one again, for
the hideous Saturday nightmare of half killing himself running
to her and then finding she wasn't there.

Until he was inside the house and had been upstairs he couldn't
rid himself of the very real hope of it. Hope doesn't die because
you tell yourself it is pointless. He dropped the food on to the

iron-legged table and lifted the phone. Then, before he dialled, he saw that the golf clubs were standing up, resting once more against the wall. But he'd kicked them over and left them in a scattered heap . . . So she had been there? Five-O-eight, then the four digits. He let the bell ring twenty times and then he put the receiver back, resolving to keep calm, to be reasonable and not to try her number again for two hours.

She'd said Tuesday but she hadn't said anything about getting in touch with him before she came. And there were all sorts of explanations to account for her absence from Combe Park. She might even have gone to the airport to meet him and they had missed each other. He went out into the front garden and lay down in the bracken. It was slightly less stuffy than the house, slightly less claustrophobic. But the atmosphere, thick, still, warm, was charged with the tension characteristic of such weather. It was as if the weather itself were waiting for something to happen.

No birds sang. The only sound was that of the flies' muted buzzing as they rose and fell in their living clouds. And the trees stood utterly immobile around the hovel, their green cloaks motionless, their trunks like pillars of stone. He lay in the bracken thinking about her, crushing down each doubt as it rose, telling himself how resolute she was, how punctual, how she never changed her mind. The front door was ajar so that he would hear the phone when it rang. He lay on his side, staring through the bracken trunks, through this forest in miniature, towards the lane, so that he would see the silver body of her car when it slid into the gap between thrusting fronds and hanging leaves. Presently, because it was warm and he had lulled himself into peace, he slept.

When he awoke it was nearly half-past five but the appearance of the Forest and the light were unchanged. No car had come and the phone hadn't rung. Half-past five was the last safe time to ring her. He went slowly back into the house and dialled but still there was no answer. All day long she'd been out, for the whole of this day when she was due to leave her husband for her lover, she'd been out. Those reassuring excuses for her absence, her silence, which had lulled him to sleep began to grow faint and a kind of dread to replace them. I never change my mind, she'd said, I'll leave Tiny and come and live with you. Tuesday, she'd said, when you get back. But she'd also said goodbye. She'd never said that before. Two or three hundred times they'd talked to each other on the phone; they'd met hundreds of times, but she'd never terminated their conversations or their meetings with a true farewell. See you, take care, till tomorrow, but never goodbye . . .

But wherever she was, whatever she'd been doing all day, she'd be bound to go home in the evening. Tiny demanded her presence in the evenings except when he was out on Thursdays. Well, he'd try again at six thirty and to hell with Tiny. He'd try every half hour throughout the evening. If she hadn't come, of course. There was always the possibility she'd promised Tiny to wait till he came home before leaving.

Although he hadn't eaten since he left Le Petit Trianon, he wasn't hungry and he didn't fancy starting on the wine he'd bought. Even the idea of a cup of tea didn't attract him. He lay back in the chair, watching the inscrutable phone, chain-smoking, lighting, smoking and crushing out five cigarettes in the hour that passed.

Tiny'd have been in half an hour by now. Whatever happened, unless he was away on a business trip—and if he'd been going away she'd have said—Drusilla's husband drove the Bentley through the Combe Park gates just before six. Perhaps he'd answer the phone. So well and good. He, Gray, would say who he was, give his name and ask to speak to Drusilla, and if Tiny wanted to know why he'd tell him why, tell him the lot. The time for discretion was past. Five-O-eight . . . He must have made a mess of it, for all he got was a steady high-pitched burr. Try again. Probably his hand hadn't been very steady. Five-O-eight . . .

The bell rang, twice, three times, twenty times. Combe Park was empty, they were both out. But it wasn't possible she'd go out with her husband, the husband she was on the point of leaving, on the very day he and she were due to start their life together.

"I love you. If you still want me I'll leave Tiny and come and live with you. As soon as you get back, soon, Tuesday . . ."

He went to the window. Standing there, gazing through a web

of unmoving, pendulous branches, he thought I won't look out of the window again till I've counted a hundred. No, I'll make a cup of tea and smoke two cigarettes and count a hundred and then she'll be here. He'd do what he'd thought of her as doing while she waited for him on Saturday.

But instead of going into the kitchen, he sat down once more in the chair and, closing his eyes, began to count. It was years since he'd counted up so high, not since he was a little boy playing hide and seek. And he didn't stop when he reached a hundred, but went obsessively on, as if he were counting the days of his life or the trees of the Forest. At a thousand he stopped and opened his eyes, frightened by what was happening to his mind, to himself. It was still only seven o'clock. He lifted the phone and dialled the number that was more familiar to him than his own, making the movements that were so automatic now that he could have made them in the dark. And the bell rang as if it were echoing his counting, on and on, emptily, pointlessly, meaninglessly.

Tiny must have taken her away. She'd told Tiny and he, aghast and angry, had shut up the house and taken away his wife from the lures of a predatory young lover. To St. Tropez or St. Moritz, to the tourists' shrines where miracles took place and in the glamour of high life women forgot the life they had left behind. He dropped the receiver and pushed his hand across his eyes, his forehead. Suppose they were away for weeks, months? There seemed no way to find out where they'd gone. He couldn't very well go questioning the neighbours and he didn't know Tiny's office number or her father's address. The thought came to him horribly that if she died no one would tell him; no news of her illness, her death, could reach him, for nobody in her circle knew of his existence and no one in his knew of hers.

There was nothing he could do but wait—and hope. After all, it was still Tuesday. She hadn't said *when* on Tuesday. Perhaps she'd postponed telling Tiny till the last minute, was telling him now, and their quarrel was so intense, their emotions running so high, that they scarcely heard the phone, still less bothered to answer it. In a little while she'd have said all there was to say and then she'd fling out of the house, throw her packed cases into the car, drive furiously down the Forest roads . . .

He was seeing it all, following the phases of their quarrel, the two angry frightened people in their beautiful loveless house, when the phone, so dead and silent that he had thought it would never ring again, gave its preliminary hiccup. His heart turned over. He had the receiver to his ear before the end of the first peal and he was holding his breath, his eyes closed.

"Mr. Graham Lanceton?"

Tiny. Could it be Tiny? The voice was thick, uncultured, but very steady. "Yes," Gray said, clenching his free hand.

The voice said, "My name is Ixworth, Detective Inspector Ixworth. I should like to come over and see you if that's convenient."

The anticlimax was so great, so sickening—far worse than when he had answered Honoré's phone to M. Reville—that Gray could hardly speak. It was as hard to find words as to find, from his dry constricted throat, the voice with which to speak them. "I don't . . ." he began thinly. "Who . . . ? What . . . ?"

"Detective Inspector Ixworth, Mr. Lanceton. Shall we say nine o'clock?"

Gray didn't answer. He didn't say anything. He put the phone down and stood shivering. It was fully five minutes before he could get over the shock of simply realising it hadn't been she. Then, wiping the sweat off his forehead, he made his way towards the kitchen where at least he'd be out of the sight of that phone.

On the threshold he stopped dead. The window had been broken and forced open and the cellar door stood ajar. All his papers were now stacked in as neat a pile as a new ream of typing paper. Someone had been here and not she. Someone had broken into the house. He shook himself, trying to get a grip on reason, on normalcy. Vaguely he began to understand the reason for that policeman's phone call. The police had discovered a burglary.

Well, he had to fill in the time till she phoned or came, and he might as well look round to see if anything had been pinched. It would be something to do. His typewriter was still there, though he had a feeling it had been moved. He couldn't remember where he'd left the strongbox. Having searched the downstairs rooms, he went up to the bedrooms. Everywhere smelt musty, airless. He opened windows as he went across the landing and his own bedroom but there was no breeze to blow stale air out and fresh in.

There was no fresh air. He longed to draw into his lungs great gulps of oxygen—something to relieve this tightness in his chest. But when he put his head out of the window the thick atmosphere seemed to stick at the rim of his throat.

The strongbox wasn't in either of the bedrooms. He no longer retained much faith in his own memory, but he was certain he'd left the box somewhere in the house. What else would he have done with it? If it wasn't there, the intruder must have taken it. He searched the "lounge" again and the kitchen and then went down the cellar steps.

Someone had disturbed and turned over those mounds of rubbish and the iron was gone. Its trivet stood on a heap of damp newspapers but the iron which had burnt him, which had left a still clearly visible scar on his hand, had disappeared. He kicked some of the coal aside, mystified by this strange robbery, and saw at his feet on the moist flagstones, a spattered brown stain.

The stain looked as if it might be blood. He remembered Dido again and thought that perhaps she'd succeeded in getting into the cellar and had fallen from the steps or wounded herself against one of the oil drums or the old unusable bicycle. It was an ugly thought that made him wince and he went quickly back up the steps. The box wasn't there, anyway.

The garden was crushed now by rising mist, cottony white and oppressive, hanging immobile on nettle and fern bract. The broken window made the kitchen look more derelict than ever. He put the kettle on for tea but he went out of the kitchen while he waited for it to boil. After what had happened there, he was never going to be able to bear that kitchen for long. Dido's ghost would be behind him. He'd fancy he could hear her padding steps or the touch of her moist nose against his hand.

Shivering, he reached for the phone again and dialled carefully but fast. They said that if you dialled too slowly or left too long a pause between two of the digits, something could go wrong and you'd get the wrong number. They said a hair across the mechanism or a grain of dust . . . suppose he'd been dialling the wrong number all this time? It could happen, some Freudian slip could make it happen. He put the receiver back, lifted it again, and dialled with calculated precision, repeating the seven figures over to himself aloud. The ringing began, and yet from the first double peal he knew it would be useless. Give up now till ten. Try again at ten and at midnight. If they weren't there at midnight he'd know they were away.

He'd made a cup of tea and carried it into the "lounge"—for all his resolve, he couldn't bear to be more than a yard from that phone—when he heard the soft purr of a car. At last. At last at twenty past eight, a perfectly reasonable time, she'd come to him. The long and terrible waiting was over, and like all long and terrible waiting times would be forgotten immediately now that what he had waited for had happened. He wouldn't run to the door, he wouldn't even look out of the window. He'd wait till the bell rang and then he'd go there slowly, hoping he could maintain this calm façade even when he saw her, white and gold and vital in the closing twilight, keep his rushing emotion down until she was in his arms.

The bell rang. Gray set down his teacup. It rang again. Oh, Drusilla, at last . . . ! He opened the door. Appalled, every muscle of his body flexing into rigidity, he stared, for it was Tiny who stood there. In every imagined detail—now proved correct by the too real reality—this man was Drusilla's husband. From the black curly hair, cropped too short and crowning, with coarse contrast, a veined dusky-red face, to the gingery suede shoes, this was Tiny Janus. He wore a white raincoat, belted slackly over a belly made thick with rich living.

They eyed each other in a silence which seemed immeasurable but which probably lasted no more than a few seconds. At first Gray, by instinct rather than by thought, had supposed the man was going to strike him. But now he saw that the mouth, which had been so grim and so belligerent, was curling into an expression of mockery, too faint to be called a smile. He stepped back, losing his sense of conviction, because the words he was hearing were wrong, were the last conceivable words in these circumstances.

"I'm a bit early." A foot over the threshold, a briefcase swung. "Nothing wrong, I hope?"

Everything was wrong, everything unbalanced. "I wasn't expecting . . ." Gray began.

"But I phoned you. My name's Ixworth."

Gray held himself still, then nodded. He pulled the door wider to admit the policeman. There is a limit to how long anticlimaxes remain anticlimactic. One grows to accept them, to take them as part and parcel of nightmare. It was better, probably, that this man should be anyone but Tiny, intolerable, just the same, that his caller was anyone but Drusilla.

"Just got back from France, have you?" They had got themselves into the "lounge"—Gray hardly knew how—and Ixworth moved confidently as if he were familiar with the place.

"Yes, I was in France." He had spoken mechanically, had simply answered the question, but there must have been in his reply some note of surprise.

"We talk to friends and neighbours, Mr. Lanceton. That's our job. All part of the job of investigating this sort of thing. You went to France to see your mother before she died, isn't that it?"

"Yes."

"Your mother died on Friday and you came home on a flying visit on Saturday, going back again that same night. You must have had a very pressing reason for that trip."

"I thought," said Gray, remembering, recalling the least significant shocks of the day, "you came to talk about my house being broken into."

"Your house?" The thick black eyebrows went up. "I understood this cottage was the property of a Mr. Warriner who is at present in Japan."

Gray shrugged. "I live here. He lent it to me. Anyway, there's nothing missing." Why mention the strongbox, when to mention it would only keep the man here? "I didn't see anyone. I wasn't here."

"You were here on Saturday afternoon."

"Only for about half an hour. Nobody'd been here then. The window wasn't broken."

"We broke the window, Mr. Lanceton," said Ixworth with a slight cough. "We entered this house with a warrant yesterday and found the body of a man lying at the foot of the cellar steps.

He'd been dead for forty-eight hours. The wristwatch he was wearing had broken and the hands stopped at four fifteen."

Gray, who had been standing limply but with a kind of slack indifferent impatience, lowered himself into the brown armchair. Or, rather, the chair seemed to rise and receive him into its lumpy uneven seat. The stunning effect of what Ixworth had said blanked his mind, but into this blankness came a vision of a little man prowling round the hovel garden.

The burglar or burglars, the brown stain . . . Who were these intruders who had forced their way into his own nightmare and made, with a kind of incongruous subplot, a littler yet greater nightmare of their own?

"This man," he said, because he had to say something, "must have fallen down the steps."

"He fell, yes." Ixworth was looking at him narrowly, as if he expected so much more than Gray could give. "He fell after he'd been struck on the head with a flatiron."

Gray looked down at his right hand, at the blister which had become a cracked and yellow callus. He turned his hand downwards when he saw that Ixworth was looking at it too.

"Are you saying this man was killed here? Who was he?"

"You don't know? Come outside a minute." The policeman led him into the kitchen, as if the house were his, as if Gray had never been there before. He opened the cellar door, watching Gray. The switch for the cellar light didn't work, and it was in the thin pale glow from the kitchen that they looked down into the depths and at the brown stain.

It was strange that he should feel so threatened, so impelled to be defensive, when none of this was anything to do with him. Or was it a case of any man's death diminishes me? All he found to say was, "He fell down those steps."

"Yes."

Suddenly Gray found he didn't like the man's tone, the expectancy, the accusatory note in it. It was almost as if Ixworth were trying to tease him into some sort of admission; as if, fantastically, the police could do no more unless he confessed to some defection or omission of his own—that he hadn't, for instance, taken proper precautions against this kind of thing or was deliberately failing to give vital information.

"I know nothing about it. I can't even imagine why he'd come here."

"No? You don't see any attractions in a charming little weather-board cottage set in unspoilt woodland?"

Gray turned away, sickened at this inept description. He didn't want to know any more, he couldn't see the point. The intruder's identity or business were nothing to him, his death an ugliness Ixworth seemed to use only as an excuse for curious glances and cryptic words. And Ixworth had been so suave, so teasing, that Gray felt a jolt shake him when, after a brief silence, the police-man spoke with a clipped brutality.

"Why did you come home on Saturday?"

"It was because of a dog," Gray said.

"A *dog*?"

"Yes. D'you think we could go back into the other room?" He wondered why he was asking Ixworth's permission. The policeman nodded and closed the cellar door. "I went to France, forgetting that someone had left a dog, a yellow Labrador, shut up in my kitchen. When I realised what I'd done, I phoned a friend from France and got them to let the dog out and take her to a vet." Si-lently, Gray blessed English usage which permitted him to say "them" instead of "her" in this context. Drusilla wouldn't thank him for involving her in all this. "It was a stupid mistake to make." Suddenly he saw just how stupid all this would sound to some-one else. "The dog died," he went on, "but—well, before that, on Saturday, the vet wanted to see me. He's called Cherwell and he lives at 21 George Street, Leyton."

Ixworth wrote the address down. "You spoke to him?"

"I couldn't find him. I spoke to a woman at 49 George Street, Leyton*stone*. That would have been just after three."

"You aren't making yourself very clear, Mr. Lanceton. Why did you go to Leytonstone?"

"I made a mistake about that."

"You seem to make a lot of mistakes."

Gray shrugged. "It doesn't matter, does it? The point is I didn't get here till six."

"*Six*? What were you doing all that time? Did you have a meal, meet anyone? If you left Leytonstone at half-past three, a bus or buses would have got you here in three quarters of an hour."

Gray said more sharply, "It's a long walk and I can't afford taxis. Besides, I went back into London and caught a train."

"Did you meet anyone, talk to anyone at all?"

"I don't think so. No, I didn't. When I got here I spoke to an old boy called Tringham who lives up the lane."

"We've interviewed Mr. Tringham. It was five past six when he spoke to you, so that doesn't help much."

"No?" said Gray. "Well, I can't help at all."

"You haven't, for instance, any theory of your own?"

"Well, there were two men, weren't there? There must have been. Mr. Tringham said he saw another bloke."

"Yes, he told us." Ixworth spoke casually, laconically, returning to his old manner. Once more it was as if he had ceased to take Gray seriously. "The Forest," he said, "is full of picnickers at this time of year."

"But surely you ought to find the other man?"

"I think we should, Mr. Lanceton." Ixworth got up. "Don't you worry, we shall. In the meantime, you won't go popping off to France again, will you?"

"No," said Gray, surprised. "Why should I?"

He saw the policeman to the gate. When his car lights had died away, the Forest was impenetrably black. And the moonless, starless sky was densely black except on the horizon where the lights of London stained it a dirty smoky red.

It was nearly ten o'clock. Gray made tea, and as he drank it the interview with Ixworth, irritating and humiliating rather than alarming, began to fade, becoming a distant instead of a recent memory. It seemed less real now than those dreams of his, for that which supremely mattered had returned to engulf him.

The light bulb in the "lounge," one of the last in the hovel that still worked, flickered, shone briefly with a final bold radiance, fizzed and went out. He had to dial her number in the dark but it was as he'd thought, his fingers slipped automatically into the right slots.

There was no reply, and none at midnight when he tried for the last time and Tuesday was over.

CHAPTER 18

Gray and Tiny and Drusilla were travelling together in a tourist coach along a road that led through a thick dark forest. The husband and wife sat in front and Gray behind them. She wore her cream lawn dress and on her finger the amethyst ring. Her hair was a red flower, a chrysanthemum with fiery points to its petals. He touched her shoulder and asked her how she came to be wearing the ring she'd sold but she took no notice, she couldn't hear him.

The forest thinned and opened on to a plain. He knew they were in France from the road signs, but when they came to Bajon it wasn't the Écu outside which they stopped but the Oranmore in Sussex Gardens. In one hand Tiny held the case containing his coin collection, with the other he grasped a passive and meek Drusilla, shepherding her up the steps, under the neon sign and into the hotel. He was going to follow them in but the glass doors slid closed against him and, although he beat on the glass begging to be admitted, Drusilla turned her head only once before going up the stairs. She turned her head once and said, "Goodbye, Gray. Goodbye."

After that he woke up and couldn't get to sleep again. Soft hazy sunshine filled the room. It was half-past eight. He got up and looked out of the window. The mist was still there but thin now, diaphanous, shot through with shafts of gold and veiling a blue sky.

Gradually the events of the previous day came back to him, the events and the non-events. He stretched, shivered, quite unrefreshed by his eight hours of uneasy, dream-filled sleep. He went downstairs. The kitchen was beginning to fill with leaf-filtered sunshine and for the first time it didn't smell stale. Fresh air came in with the sunlight through the broken window. Gray put the kettle on. It was strange, he thought, how, since Christmas, day had followed day without anything ever happening in a terrible monotony, and then had come a week filled with ugly violent action. Wasn't it Kafka who'd said, no matter how you lock yourself away, shut yourself up, life will come and roll in ecstasy at your feet? Well, it was hardly ecstasy, anything but. And it was very far from the kind of life and ecstasy he'd envisaged.

He couldn't see how the intruders had got in. The doors had been locked and the spare key hanging at that time over the sink. Probably the police wouldn't bother him any more now they knew he hadn't been here and couldn't assist them. Strange to remember how bitterly disappointed he'd been at not finding Drusilla here on Saturday. He was glad now, he thanked God, she hadn't been here when the men had broken in.

He'd try her number just once more and if he got no reply think of ways and means to get hold of her. Why not ask her neighbours, after all? Someone would know where she and Tiny had gone. The daily woman would come in whether they were there or not and she'd be bound to know. He dialled the number just before nine, listened this time without much disappointment and no surprise to the ringing tone, put the receiver back and made tea. While he was eating some of the bread he'd bought, spreading it with vinegar-tainted melting butter, the phone rang.

It must be she. Who else would know he was home? He gulped down a mouthful of bread and answered it.

A woman's voice, a voice he didn't begin to recognise, said, "Mr. Lanceton? Mr. Graham Lanceton?"

"Yes," he said dully.

"Oh, *hallo*, Graham! It didn't sound a bit like you. This is Eva Warriner."

Mal's mother. What did she want? "How are you, Mrs. Warriner?"

"I'm fine, my dear, but I was so distressed to hear about your mother. It was nice of you to write to me. I'd no idea she was as ill as that. We were very close in the old days, I always thought of her as one of my dearest friends. I hope she didn't suffer much?"

Gray didn't know what to say. It was a struggle to speak at all, to make a recovery from the bitterness of knowing this wasn't Drusilla. "She did for a while," he managed. "She didn't know me."

"Oh, dear, so sad for you. You said you'd be back at the beginning of the week so I just thought I'd phone and tell you how sorry I am. Oh, and I rang Isabel Clarion and told her the news too. She said she hadn't heard from you at all."

"*Isabel?*" he almost shouted. "You mean she's come back from Australia already?"

"Well, yes, Graham," said Mrs. Warriner, "she must have. She didn't mention Australia but we only talked for a couple of minutes. The builders that are doing her flat were making so much noise we couldn't hear ourselves speak."

He sat down heavily, pushing his fingers across his hot damp forehead. "I expect I'll hear from her," he said weakly.

"I'm sure you will. Isn't it wonderful Mal coming home in August?"

"Yes. Yes, it's great. Er—Mrs. Warriner, Isabel didn't say anything about . . . ? No, it doesn't matter."

"She hardly said anything, Graham." Mrs. Warriner began to reminisce about her past friendship with Enid but Gray cut her short as soon as he politely could and said goodbye. He didn't replace the receiver but left it hanging as it had so often hung in the past. That would stop Isabel for a while, at any rate, Isabel who'd stayed in Australia for barely a week. Probably she'd quarrelled with her old partner or hadn't liked the climate or something. Vaguely he remembered reading in Honoré's newspaper, on that dreadful night when he'd realised Dido was at the hovel, about floods in Australia. That would be it. Isabel had been frightened or made uncomfortable by those floods and had got on a plane as soon as she could. She'd very likely got home yesterday and today she'd want her dog back . . .

Well, he'd known he'd have to tell her sometime and it would be as well to get it over. But not today. Today he had to sort out his life and Drusilla's, find where Drusilla was and get her back. He eyed the receiver that was still swinging like a pendulum. Better make one more attempt to phone. By now the daily woman would have arrived.

Five-O-eight and then the four digits. The double burrs began. After the fifth the receiver was lifted. Gray held his breath, the fingers of his left hand curling into the palm and the nails biting the flesh. It wasn't she. Still, it was someone, a human voice coming out of that silent place at last.

"Combe Park."

"I'd like to talk to Mrs. Janus."

"Mrs. Janus is away. This is the cleaner. Who's that speaking?"

"When will she be back?"

"I'm sure I couldn't tell you. Who's that speaking?"

"A friend," Gray said. "Have Mr. and Mrs. Janus gone away on holiday?"

The woman cleared her throat. She said, "Oh, dear . . ." and "I don't know if I should . . ." and then, gruffly, "Mr. Janus passed away."

It didn't register. All it did was bring back a flashing memory of the mayor and his euphemisms, those idiomatic polished understatements. "What did you say?"

"Mr. Janus passed away."

He heard the words but they seemed to take a long while to travel to his brain, as such words do, as do any words that are the vehicles of news that is unimaginable.

"You mean he's dead?"

"It's not my place to talk about it. All I know is he's passed away, dead like you say, and Mrs. Janus has gone to her mum and dad."

"Dead . . ." he said and then, steadying his voice, "D'you know their address?"

"No, I don't. Who's that speaking?"

"It doesn't matter," Gray said. "Forget it."

He made his way very slowly to the window but he seemed half blind and, instead of the forest, all he saw was a blaze of sun and hollows of blue shadow. Tiny Janus is dead, said his brain. The words travelled to his lips and he spoke them aloud, wonderingly, Harvey Janus, the rich man, the ogre, is dead. Drusilla's husband is dead. The phrases, the thoughts, swelled and began to take on real meaning as the shock subsided. He began to feel them as facts. Tiny Janus, Drusilla's husband, is dead.

When had it happened? Sunday? Monday? Perhaps even on Tuesday, the day she was to join him. Now her absence was explained. Even her failure to phone was explained. Dazed but gradually coming to grips with the news, he tried to imagine what had occurred. Probably Tiny had had a coronary. Heavy fat men like Tiny, men who drank too much and lived too well, men of Tiny's age, often did have coronaries. Perhaps it had happened at his office or while he was driving the Bentley, and they had sent her a message or the police had come to her. She hadn't loved Tiny but still it would have been a shock and she would have been alone.

She'd have sent for her parents, the father she loved and the mother she never mentioned. It was hard to imagine Drusilla having a mother, Drusilla who seemed man-born. They must have carried her off to wherever they lived. He realised he didn't know their name, her maiden name, or anything about where they lived except that it was somewhere in Hertfordshire. But her failure to phone him was explained. He would just have to wait.

"Wouldn't it be nice if he died?" she'd said. "He might die. He might have a coronary or crash his car."

Well, she'd got what she wanted. Tiny was dead and Combe Park and all that money hers. He thought how she'd said that when she got it she'd give it to him, that they would share it, put it into a joint account and live happily on it forever. And he'd wanted it, if it could have been his more or less legitimately, reaching a zenith of desire for it when he'd stood outside the gates of Combe Park in the spring and seen the daffodils that seemed made of pure gold. Strange that now the impossible had happened and Tiny was dead, now it would all be his and hers, he no longer cared at all about possessing it.

He tested his feelings. No, he wasn't happy, glad that a man was dead. Of course, he had nothing to do with Tiny's death, no more than he had to do with the death of the man who had fallen down his cellar stairs, yet he felt a heavy weight descend onto his shoulders, something like despair. Was it because in his heart he'd really wanted Tiny to die? Or for some other reason he couldn't define? The two deaths seemed to merge into one and to stand between him and Drusilla like a single ghost.

His body smelt of the sweat of tension. He went back to the kitchen and began heating water for a bath. All the time he was waiting for happiness and relief to dispel his depression, but he could only think of the repeated shocks to which he'd been exposed. He couldn't take any more. Another shock would send him over the edge.

He lifted the lid of the bath cover and tugged out the tangle of mould-smelling sheets and towels. The mud-stained trousers he'd put in there on Saturday were gone but he didn't worry about their disappearance. Too many strange things were happening in his world for that. He poured the boiling water into the bathtub, chucked in a bucketful of cold. Getting into the bath, soaping himself, he thought of Tiny dead. At the wheel of his car perhaps? In so many dreams he'd seen Tiny crash in his car, blood and flames pouring scarlet over the green turf. Or had he died in bed after a drinking bout while Drusilla, unaware and dreaming of her lover, slept a yard from him?

There were many other possibilities. But the only one that came vividly to Gray, the only one he could see as a real picture, was of Tiny lying crumpled at the foot of a flight of stairs.

If he went up the lane just before twelve, he might be able to catch the milkman and buy a pint off him. Tea was the only sustenance he felt he could stomach. The food in the carrier bag smelt unpleasant, and the sight of it brought him a wave of nausea. Downstairs the hovel seemed full of death, the intruder's, Tiny's, the dog's, and yet the rooms gleamed with sunlight. Gray could never remember the place so bright and airy. But he longed to get out of it. If once he got out, would he have the courage to come back? Or would he wander through the glades of the Forest, on and on until weariness overcame him and he lay down to sleep or die?

The chance of her phoning seemed to have grown very remote. Days might pass before he heard from her. He couldn't envisage those empty days and himself passing through them, waiting, waiting, and all the time this tension mounting until, before she phoned, it cracked.

He went upstairs and put on the dirty shirt he'd taken off the night before. The sound of a car engine a long way up the lane froze him as he was combing his hair. Holding the comb poised, utterly still, he listened for the whisper of sound to grow into the powerful purr of a Jaguar sports. He'd passed beyond feeling joy at her coming. All these deaths, anticlimaxes, shocks, blows to his mind had removed the possibility of delight at their coming meeting. But he would fall into her arms and cling to her in silence when she came.

It was not to be yet. The engine noise had become the thinner jerkier rattle of a small car. He went to the window and looked out. Much of the lane was obscured by bracken at ground level and by branches above, but there was a space between wide enough to make out the shape and colour of a car. The Mini, small and bright red, edged cautiously along the still sticky surface and slid to a halt.

Isabel.

His first instinct was simply to hide from her, go into the spare room, lie on the floor and hide till she went away. Inside each one of us is a frightened child trying to get out. The measure of our maturity is the extent to which we are able to keep that child quiet, confined and concealed. At that moment the child inside Gray almost broke loose from its bonds, but the man who was nearly thirty held it down, just held it down. Isabel might go away but she'd come back. If not today, tomorrow, if not tomorrow, Friday. Weak as he was, trembling now, he must face her and tell her what he'd done. No hiding, defiance, blustering, could make his act less of an outrage than it was.

She was getting out of the car. In the bright, sun-flooded segment between dark green fern and lemon-green leaves, he saw her ease her thick body in pink blouse and baby blue trousers out of the driving seat. She was wearing big sunglasses with rainbow frames. The black circles of glass levelled themselves upwards towards the window and Gray turned quickly away.

He retreated to the door, to the top of the stairs, and there he stood, trying to command himself, clenching his hands. He was still a child. For more than half his life he'd fended for himself; he'd got a good degree, written a successful book, been Drusilla's lover, but he was still a child. And more than ever he was a child with these grown-ups, with Honoré, with dead Enid, Mrs. Warriner, Isabel. Even in telling himself he wouldn't conciliate them or play things their way but be honest and himself, he was a child, for his very defiance and rebellion were as childish as obedience. In a flash he was aware of this as never before. One day, he thought, when the present and all its horrors were the past, when he'd got over or through all this, he would remember and grow up . . .

Sick, already tasting the nausea on his tongue, he went down and slowly pulled open the front door. Isabel, still at the car, bending over to take milk and groceries out of the boot, lifted her head and waved to him. He began to walk towards her.

Before he was halfway down the path, before he could fetch a word out of his dry throat, the thicket of bracken split open. It burst with a crack like tearing sacking and the big yellow dog leapt upon him, the violence of her embrace softened by the wet warmth of her tongue and the rapture in her kind eyes.

CHAPTER 19

The bright air shivered. The myriad leaves, lemony-green, silk-green, feathery, sun-filtered, serrated, swam in swirling parabolas, and the ground rose in a hard wave to meet him. He just kept his balance. He shut his eyes on the green-gold trembling brightness and thrust his fingers into warm fur, embracing the dog, holding her against his shaking body.

"Dido!" Isabel called. "Leave Gray alone, darling."

He couldn't speak. Shock stunned him. All his feeling, all thought, were crystallised into one unbelievable phrase: she is alive, the dog is alive. He drew his hands over Dido's head, the fine bones, the modelling, as a blind man passes his fingers over the face of the woman he loves.

"Are you all right, Gray? You do look peaky. I suppose you're just beginning to feel what this loss means."

"Loss?" he said.

"Your *mother*, dear. Mrs. Warriner told me last night and I made up my mind to come over first thing this morning. You ought to sit down. Just now I thought you were going to faint."

Gray had thought so too. And even now, when the first shock had passed, he seemed unable to get his bearings. Following Isabel into the house, he tried to feel his way along that other path that should have led into the reaches of his mind. But he came against a blank wall. Experience and memory had become a foreign country. Logic had gone, and lost too were the processes of thought by which one says, this happened so, therefore, this and this happened too. His mind was an empty page with one phrase written on it: the dog is alive. And now, slowly, another was being inscribed alongside it: the dog is alive, Tiny Janus is dead.

Isabel was already sitting down in the "lounge," pouring out platitudes on life, death, and resignation. Gray lowered himself carefully into the other chair as if his body, as well as his mind, must be guardedly handled. Speed, roughness, would be dangerous, for, lying beneath the surface was a scream that might burst out. He rubbed his hands over the dog's pelt. She was real, he knew that for certain now. Perhaps she was the only real thing in a tumbling, inside-out world.

"When all's said and done," Isabel was saying, "it was a merciful release." Gray lifted his eyes to her, to this fat pink and blue blur that was his godmother, and wondered what she was talking about. "You haven't got your receiver off now, I see. Really, there's no point in having a phone if the receiver's always off, is there?"

"No point at all," he agreed politely. He was surprised that he could speak at all, let alone form sentences. He went on doing it, pointlessly, just to prove he could. "I wonder sometimes why I do have one. I really wonder. I might just as well not have one."

"There's no need," Isabel said sharply, "to be sarcastic. You've no right to be resentful, Gray. The first thing I did was try to phone you. As soon as I knew I couldn't go to Australia—I mean, when I read about the floods and Molly cabled me to say she'd literally been washed out of her home—I made up my mind there was no point in trying to go. I tried to phone you that Friday and goodness knows how many times on the Saturday, and then I gave up in sheer despair. I thought you'd realise when I didn't turn up with Dido."

"Yes," said Gray. "Oh, yes."

"Well, then. Really, it was a blessing I didn't go to Molly's. All the responsibility of getting Dido boarded would have been on your shoulders, and you had quite enough with your poor mother, I'm sure. Lie down, darling. You're just making yourself hot. I shall write to Honoré today, poor man, and tell him I've seen you and how upset you are. It cheers people up knowing others are unhappy, don't you think?"

This crass expression of *schadenfreude*, which once would have made Gray laugh, now washed over him with most of the rest of Isabel's words. While she continued to burble, he sat as still as stone, his hands no longer caressing the dog who had sunk into a somnolent heap at his feet. Memory was beginning to come back now, returning in hard thrusts of pain.

"Is she dead?" he'd asked, relying on her, utterly in her hands.

"No, she was alive—just."

His hand fell again to fumble at the dog's coat, to feel her reality. And Dido turned her head, opened her eyes and licked his hand.

"I took some milk and chicken with me. I was a bit scared to open the kitchen door but I needn't have been. She was too weak to move. Someone ought to lock you up in a cell and see how you'd like it."

Oh, Drusilla, Drusilla . . .

"It's no use, anyway, the dog's had to be destroyed."

Oh, Dru, no . . .

"Anyway, dear," said Isabel, drawing breath, "you can have your key back now. Here you are. I'll go and hang it on the hook, shall I?"

"I'll take it."

An old blackened key, twin of the one he always carried.

"And put the kettle on, Gray. I brought some milk in case you didn't have any. We'll have a cup of tea and I'll run into Waltham Abbey and get us something for our lunch. I'm sure you're not fit to take care of yourself."

Not fit . . .

"I went in and cleaned up for you," she'd said.

"Why did you do that?"

"Why do I do anything for you? Don't you know yet?"

The bright key that had been Drusilla's hung on the hook, glittering like gold in the sun. She'd left her key and said goodbye. Alone, free of Isabel for a moment, he laid his face, his forehead, against the damp cold wall and the scream came out into the stone, agonising, uncomprehending, silent.

"I love you. If you still want me I'll leave Tiny and come and live with you."

I love you . . . No, he whispered, no, no. Goodbye, Gray, goodbye. I never change my mind. Punctual, relentless, unchanging in any fixed course, she never wavered. But this . . . ? Red fur, red fox hair, perfume rising like smoke, that low throaty laugh of hers —the memories spun, crystallised into a last image of her, as hard and unyielding as the stone against his face.

"A watched pot never boils, dear," said Isabel brightly from the doorway. She peered inquisitively at his numb blind face. "There's a car pulled up at your gate. Are you expecting anyone?"

He had been so adept at optimism, at supposing with uncrushable hope that every car was hers, every phone bell ringing to bring her to him. This time he had no hope and, in realising his deep stunned hopelessness, he knew too that he was living reality. He'd never see her again. She'd left her key and said goodbye. Betraying him systematically and coldly for perhaps some purpose of revenge, she'd brought him to this climax. Without speaking, he pushed past Isabel and opened the door to Ixworth. He gazed speechlessly but without dismay or even surprise at the policeman whose coming seemed the next natural and logical step in this sequence of happenings. He didn't speak because he had nothing to say and felt now that all words would be wasted effort. Why talk when event would now, in any case, pile upon event according to the pattern she had designed for them?

Ixworth looked at the flattened bracken. "Been sunbathing?"

Gray shook his head. This, then, was what it felt like to have the mental breakdown he'd feared all those months. Not manic hysteria, not fantasy unbridled or grief too strong to bear, but this peaceful numb acceptance of fate. After the liberating silent scream, just acceptance. It was possible even to believe that in a moment he would feel almost happy . . . Gently he held the dog back to keep her from springing lovingly at Ixworth.

"*Another* yellow Labrador, Mr. Lanceton? D'you breed them?"

"It's the same dog." Gray didn't trouble to consider the implication of his words. He turned away, indifferent as to whether Ixworth followed him or not, and almost collided with Isabel who was saying in sprightly tones, "Aren't you going to introduce me?"

Grotesquely girlish, she fluttered in front of the dour inspector. Gray said, "Miss Clarion, Mr. Ixworth." He wished vaguely that they would both go away. If only they would go away and leave him with the dog. He'd lie down somewhere with kind Dido, put his arms round her, bury his face in her warm, hay-scented fur.

Ixworth ignored the introduction. "Is that your dog?"

"Yes, isn't she gorgeous? Are you fond of dogs?"

"This one seems attractive." Ixworth's eyes flickered over Gray. "Is this the animal you were supposed to be looking after?"

"I'm sure he will when I do finally go away." Isabel seemed delighted that the conversation was taking such a pleasant sociable turn. "This time my trip fell through and poor Dido didn't get her country holiday."

"I see. I rather hoped I'd find you alone, Mr. Lanceton."

Quick to warm, equally quick to take offence, Isabel tossed her head and stubbed out her cigarette fiercely. "Please don't let me intrude. The last thing I want is to be in the way. I'll run into Waltham Abbey now, Gray, and get our lunch. I wouldn't dream of keeping you from your friend."

Ixworth smiled slightly at this. He waited in patient silence till the Mini had gone.

Gray watched the car move off down the lane. Dido began to whine, her paws on the windowsill, her nose pressed against the glass. This, Gray thought, was how it must have been when Isabel left her alone here that Monday . . . Only that had never happened, had it? None of that had happened.

"None of that really happened, did it?" Ixworth was saying. "Your whole story about the dog was untrue. We know, of course, that no animal answering this one's description was ever taken to Mr. Cherwell on Thursday."

Gray pulled the dog down gently. The sun's glare hurt his eyes and he pulled the chair away from the slanting dazzling rays. "Does it matter?" he said.

"Tell me," said the policeman in a tone which was both puzzled and bantering, "what you think does matter."

Nothing much now, Gray thought. Perhaps just one or two small things, questions to which he couldn't supply the answers himself. But his brain was clearing, revealing cold facts to which he seemed to have no emotional reaction. The dog had never been there. Working onwards from that, recalling certain phrases of hers in this new context—"I never change my mind, Gray"—he began to see the pattern she had designed. He saw it without pain, dully, almost scientifically. "I thought," he said, "that Harvey Janus was a big man but then I'd never seen him, and I thought he had a Bentley still, not the Mercedes he left in the lane. Strange, I suppose they called him Tiny because he *was* tiny. Would you like some tea?"

"Not now. Right now I'd like you to go on talking."

"There was no need to drug him, of course. I see that now. It was only necessary to get him here. That was easy because he was looking for a house in the Forest to buy his mother. And easy to overpower such a small man. Anyone could have done it."

"Oh, yes?"

"She had her key then. But I don't quite see . . ." He paused, sticking at betraying her even though she'd betrayed him. "But I suppose you've talked to Mrs. Janus? Even . . ." He sighed, though there was very little feeling left to make him sigh.

"Even arrested her?" he said.

Ixworth's face changed. It hardened, grew tough like that of some cinema cop. He reached for his briefcase and opened it, taking out a sheet of paper from a thin file. The paper fluttered in the sunbeam as he held it out to Gray. The typed words danced but Gray could read them. He'd typed them himself.

His address was at the top: *The White Cottage, Pocket Lane, Waltham Abbey, Essex.* Underneath that was the date: *June the sixth.* No year. And at the foot, under those terrible words he'd thought he'd never see again: *Harvey Janus Esq., Combe Park, Wintry Hill, Loughton, Essex.*

"Have you read it?"

"Oh, yes, I've read it."

But Ixworth read it aloud to him, just the same.

" 'Dear Sir, In reply to your advertisement in *The Times*, I think I have just what you are looking for. Since my home is not far from yours, would you care to come over and see it? Four o'clock on Saturday would be a suitable time. Yours faithfully, Francis Duval.' "

The letter was the first they'd written.

"Where did you find it?" Gray asked. "Here? In this house?"

"It was in his breast pocket," said Ixworth.

"It *can't* have been. It was never posted. Look, I'll try to explain . . ."

"I wish you would."

"It's very difficult to explain. Mrs. Janus . . ." He didn't wince at her name but he hesitated, searching for a form into which to fit his sentence. "Mrs. Janus," he began again, wondering why Ixworth was frowning, "will have told you we were close friends.

At one time she wanted me to . . ." How to describe what she'd wanted to this hard-faced inscrutable judge? How make him understand where fantasy ended and reality began? ". . . to play a trick on her husband," he said, lying awkwardly, "to get money from him. She had no money of her own and I'm always broke."

"We are aware of the state of your finances."

"Yes, you seem to be aware of everything. I did write that letter. I wrote a whole lot more which were never sent and I've still got them. They're . . ."

"Yes?"

"I burnt them. I remember now. But that one must have got . . . Why are you looking at me like that? Mrs. Janus . . ."

Ixworth took the letter and refolded it. "I thought we were really getting somewhere, Lanceton, till you brought Mrs. Janus's name up. Leave her out of this. She doesn't know you. She's never heard of you either as Duval or Lanceton."

The dog moved away from him. It seemed symbolic. She lay down and snored softly. Ixworth hadn't stopped talking. Steadily, he was outlining details of the events of Saturday afternoon. They were precise circumstantial details and they included his, Gray's, arrival at the hovel just before four, his greeting of Tiny Janus, their subsequent journey round the house and to the head of the cellar stairs. There was nothing wrong with the account except that it was inaccurate in every particular.

But Gray didn't deny it. He said flatly, "She doesn't know me."

"Leave her out of it. On Saturday afternoon she was playing tennis with the man who coaches her."

"We were lovers for two years," Gray said. "She's got a key to this house." No, that wasn't true any more . . . "Does she say she doesn't even know me?"

"Can you produce witnesses to prove she did?"

He was silent. There was no one. Nobody had ever seen them together so it had never happened. Their love had no more happened than the dog's death had happened. And yet . . .

Without heat or the least emotion, he said slowly, "Why would I have killed Janus except to get his wife?"

"For gain, of course," said Ixworth. "We're not children,

Lanceton. You're not a child. Credit us with a little intelligence. He was a rich man and you're a very poor one. I'll tell you frankly we have it from the French police you didn't even gain by your mother's death."

The hundred pounds . . . Had there been more hidden in the house? "He brought the deposit with him."

"Of course. You banked on that. Mr. Janus was very unwisely in the habit of carrying large sums of money on him, and these things get around, don't they? Even without seeing it, he was pretty sure he'd want this place and he was going to secure it— with cash." Ixworth shrugged, a heavy contemptuous gesture. "My God, and it wasn't even yours to sell! I suppose you worked out the sort of price it would fetch from looking in estate agents' windows."

"I know what it's worth."

"You knew what it would *fetch*, say. And you knew a good deal about human greed and need too. We found the three thousand pounds Mr. Janus brought with him in your strongbox with a copy of *The Times* and his advertisement marked. The box was locked and the key gone, but we broke it open."

Gray said, "Oh, God," very softly and hopelessly.

"I don't know if you're interested in knowing how we got on to you. It's obvious, really. Mrs. Janus knew where her husband had gone and how much money he was carrying. She reported him missing and we found his Mercedes in the lane."

Gray nodded at the inexorability, the neatness of it. "Someone ought to shut you up in a cell," she'd said. And perhaps there was a rightness in it somewhere, a harsh justice. He felt too weak, too unarmed, to argue and he knew he never would. He must accept. In writing the letters at all, he must always have hoped for an outcome of this kind; only his higher consciousness had struggled, deceiving him. He'd hoped for Tiny's death and, caught in her net, done as much as she to bring it about. Who spun, who held the scissors, and who cut the thread? Had the traffic light made his fate, or Jeff, or the buyer who hadn't got the paper in? Who made Honoré's marriage but the night phone caller? And who had made Tiny's death but he by meeting on that winter's day Tiny's wife? Who but Sir Smile, his neighbour?

"You'll want to make a statement," Ixworth said. "Shall we go?"

Gray smiled, for blank peace had returned. "If we might just wait for Miss Clarion?"

"Put the door on the latch and leave her a note." Ixworth spoke understandingly, almost sympathetically. His eye, satisfied now, no longer mocking, glanced on the sleeping Dido. "We can—er, shut the dog up in the kitchen."

AFTER

There were only six beds in the Alexander Fleming Ward. The Member hesitated in the doorway and then made for the one bed around which the curtains were drawn. But before he reached it a nurse intercepted him.

"Mr. Denman's visitors are restricted to ten minutes. He's still in a serious condition."

Andrew Laud nodded. "I won't stay long."

The nurse lifted one of the curtains for him and he ducked under it apprehensively, wondering what he was going to see. A hideously scarred face? A head swathed in bandages?

Jeff Denman said, "Thank God you could come. I've been on tenterhooks all day," and then the Member looked at him. He was as he had always been, apart from his pallor and his hair which had been cropped to within an inch of his head.

"How are you, Jeff?"

"I'm much better. I'll be O.K. It's a strange sensation to wake up in the morning and find that yesterday was six months ago."

The bed was covered with newspapers which the nurse stacked into a neat pile before swishing out through the curtains. The Member saw his own face staring out from the top one and the headline: M.P. ACTS IN FOREST MURDER APPEAL.

"I haven't acted very much," he said. "They've let me see Gray a couple of times but he seems to have a kind of amnesia about the whole thing. He either can't or won't remember. All he talks about is getting out and starting to write again but that, of course, unless this Appeal . . ."

Jeff interrupted him. "I haven't got amnesia, surprisingly enough." He shifted in the bed, lifting his head painfully from the pillow. "But first I'd better tell you how I come to be here."

"You explained that in your letter."

"I had to get the sister to write that and I couldn't get my thoughts straight. You see, when I recovered consciousness and saw the papers it was such a shock. I couldn't believe Gray had got fifteen years for murder and I dictated that letter very incoherently. I just prayed you'd take me seriously and come. Give me a drink of water, will you?"

Andrew Laud put the glass to his lips and when Jeff had drunk, said, "I've gathered that your van crashed into a lorry somewhere in Waltham Abbey on June the twelfth and you were seriously injured. As soon as I read that I knew you might have something important to tell me, but you didn't explain what you were doing there."

"My job," Jeff said. "Moving furniture, or trying to." He coughed, holding his hands to his ribs. "The Sunday before that Gray asked me to move his stuff for him on the following Saturday. He said he'd phone if anything went wrong—things are liable to go wrong for him—and when he didn't I drove over there like I promised. It was the day after I'd had that letter from you asking me to dinner. You must have wondered why I didn't accept your wife's invitation."

"Never mind that. Tell me what happened."

Jeff said slowly, but quite clearly and coherently, "I got there about three. I left the van on the metalled part of the lane because it was muddy and I thought the wheels might get stuck. When I got to the cottage there was a key in the lock and a note pinned up beside it. It was typed on Gray's typewriter—I know that typewriter—but it wasn't signed. It said something like *Have to go out for a while. Let yourself in and have a look round.* I thought it was meant for me.

"I went in, made a sort of mental note of the things he'd want me to move—which is what I thought he'd meant in the note—and sat down to wait for him. Oh, and I went all over the house. If there's any question of Gray's having been there then, I can tell you he wasn't."

"You remember everything very clearly."

"Not the accident," said Jeff, and he winced slightly. "I can't remember a thing about that. But what happened before is quite clear to me. The place was very stuffy and musty-smelling," he went on after a pause, "and when it got to be nearly four o'clock I decided to go outside again, leaving the key and the note where they were. I thought I'd sit in the garden but it was so overgrown that I went into the Forest and walked about a bit. But the point is I never went out of sight of the cottage. I was pretty fed-up with Gray by this time and I wanted to get the job over and done with as soon as he got back."

"He didn't come?"

Jeff shook his head. "I sat down under a tree. I decided to give him ten minutes and then I'd go. Well, I was sitting there when I saw two people come down the lane."

"Did you now?" The Member leaned closer towards the bed. "In a car? On foot?"

"On foot. A little short bloke of about forty and a much younger woman. They went up to the door, read the note and let themselves in. They didn't see me, I'm sure of that. I realised then that the note was meant for them, not me. And I felt very strange about that, Andy. I just didn't know what to do."

"I don't quite follow you there," said the M.P.

"I recognised the girl. I knew her. I recognised her as a former girl friend of Gray's. And I couldn't understand what she was doing there with a bloke I was somehow certain must be her husband. He *looked* like a husband. I wondered if they'd come to have some sort of a scene with Gray. No, don't interrupt, Andy. Let me tell you the rest." The sick man's voice was beginning to flag. He rested back against his pillows and gave another painful dry cough. "I can tell you precisely when and where I'd seen her before. Gray brought her back to Tranmere Villas. Sally was living with me then. Gray had forewarned her and she kept out of the way when he and this girl came in, she never even saw them. But I'd been at work, I didn't know, and I opened the door of his room without knocking as soon as I got in. There was a review of his book in the evening paper and I was so pleased I rushed in to show him. They were on the bed making love. Gray was so—well, lost, I suppose you'd say—that he didn't even know I'd come in. But she did. She looked up and smiled a sort of look-how-daring-and-clever-I-am smile. I got out as fast and quietly as I could."

Andrew Laud said over his shoulder as the curtain was drawn aside, "Just two more minutes, nurse. I promise to go in two minutes."

"Mr. Denman mustn't get excited."

"I'm the one that's getting excited, Jeff," said the Member when they were alone again. "Go back to June the twelfth now, will you?"

"Where was I? Oh, yes, sitting under that tree. After a while an old boy came along the lane, reading a book, and then the bloke I'd seen go into the cottage came out and walked around the place, looking up at the windows. I thought they were going and I waited for her to come out too. Well, the bloke went back into the house and about ten minutes later the girl came out alone. She didn't put the key back in the door and the note had gone. I thought she looked a bit shaken, Andy, and she wasn't walking very steadily. I nearly called out to her to ask if she was all right, but I didn't, though I was beginning to think the whole thing was a bit odd. She walked away into the Forest and when she'd gone I went too. I thought I'd drive down to Waltham Abbey to see if I could find Gray and tell him about it. There was a big green car parked near the van. I didn't notice the make or the number.

"It must have been about half-past four then because they tell me I had the crash at twenty to five. And that's all. Since then I've been asleep and what I've told you has been asleep with me. Christ, suppose I'd died?"

"You didn't, and you won't now. You'll have to get well fast so that you can tell all that to the Appeal Court. It's a pity you don't know who the girl was."

"But I do. Didn't I say?" Jeff was lying down now, exhausted, his face grey. But he spoke with a feeble intensity. "I'd know that face anywhere and I saw it again yesterday. There was a picture in the paper of Mrs. Drusilla Janus, or Mrs. McBride, as I suppose I should call her. The *Standard* said she got married to some tennis coach last month. You'll have to go now, Andy. Keep in touch?"

Smiling, a little dazed, the Member got up. Jeff reached out from under the bedclothes and, silently, rather formally, the two men shook hands.

DATE DUE